Swede

Become Your Best!

Caron

Maynard

SKYE **3** SERIES

Swede

by

CAROL DUERKSEN & MAYNARD KNEPP

WILLOWSPRING DOWNS

Swede
Book 3 — Skye Series
Copyright © 2000 by WillowSpring Downs

First Printing, 2000

Printed in the United States of America

Cover illustration by Susan Bartel

Page design & layout by Good Shepherd Publications,
Newton, Kansas. Web site: www.gspbooks.com

Library of Congress Catalog Number 00-101939
ISBN 0-9648525-9-4

ACKNOWLEDGMENTS

The following friends and family members were invaluable in making *Swede* a reality. They supported and encouraged us, critiqued the manuscript, and shared their time and expertise. Thank you so much to:

Sharon Hubbard
Lisa Axman
Laurie L. Oswald
Cindy Schmidt
Milton & Alice Duerksen
Annika Schulze
Marie Osland

Mary Lou Farmer
Madelene Svensson
Leanne Githens
Marlo Duerksen
Gary Duerksen
Landon Jordan

PROLOGUE

IF HE HADN'T been sitting in a place full of eyes and ears, Henrik Svensson might have cried. But the rule was, 18-year-old guys didn't cry in front of people. He stared out the window from seat 7A, his dark glasses hiding the sadness in his eyes. If only the plane would leave so he couldn't see them all watching from the airport window. If only the plane wouldn't leave, and he'd have to stay.

The tall man on the left—the one in the black Harley Davidson T-shirt and black jeans. Bo. He hadn't changed a bit since Henrik first saw him ten months ago. Same airport, same clothes, same deep "Hello Henrik" voice. The woman standing next to him, her arm around his waist, hadn't changed either. He'd been impressed with Bo's wife, Skye, the minute he'd stepped off the plane. Beautiful, trim and tan, she could be Swedish with her long blond hair and green eyes. Okay, she was old enough to be his mother, but she was 100 percent cool. And then, next to Skye. . .

The plane was moving. The figures at the window blurred and faded. His eyes swimming, Henrik pulled a faded red bandanna from his pocket. Staring down at the bandanna in his hands, Henrik nearly broke. He leaned against the window, closed his eyes, and gave in to the flood of memories washing over him.

ONE

HENRIK did not want to be an exchange student. That his older brother and sisters had done it was enough to make him think twice, even though they'd all had a great time. They came back to Sweden full of praise for the exchange program and their experiences in the United States. It was just that Henrik didn't always want to follow in their footsteps. He was tired of everyone assuming he would continue the Svensson tradition. His ancestors were the founding family of Svensund and of a very successful lumber and furniture business. Now his father owned it, and his brother was working for him. Henrik wasn't at all convinced that he should go to America to perfect his English, and someday become the company sales representative. Maybe he just wanted to chase women, party, travel. Live, for God's sake. It seemed to him that his family was too busy to enjoy life.

"It's a stage he's going through," he heard his parents say. He knew they hoped that the exchange program would help him grow up, give him some boundaries. In America, the organization wouldn't allow him to do some of the things he did in Sweden.

In the end, he agreed to apply because he was tired of the pressure. Ten months wasn't that long. With a little ingenuity, he could probably find a way to do what he wanted and not get caught. And besides, there were the American girls to check out.

The interview that determined his acceptance into the program was conducted by a small, dark-haired man. He looked across the table at Henrik with a faint smile.

"So, Henrik, why do you want to go to the United States as an exchange student?"

"Chase broads."

"Excuse me?"

"Because it will broaden my awareness of the world. I want to experience another culture, and improve my English." Ask a predictable question and you get a predictable answer.

"And how open are you to other cultures? For example, would be you willing to live with an African-American family?"

"Sure. I know I can trust your judgment to find me a good family," Henrik grinned. "Just no hillbillies, okay?"

"Meaning ...?"

"Just joking." The man has no sense of humor.

"You realize that you could be placed anywhere in the United States?"

"Yes. Of course, I'd prefer California where the babes are."

The look on the interviewer's face clearly indicated to Henrik that his flippant remarks were jeopardizing his opportunity to become an exchange student. He leaned forward and looked the man in the eye.

"I'm sorry. That was a joke, too. I will be serious from now on."

"I certainly hope so. Your acceptance into the program depends on my impression of your sincerity."

"Yes, sir. I understand."

"Tell me about a time when you had to be flexible and adjust to something new," the interviewer said, tapping his pen on the table.

Henrik pushed his blond hair off his forehead, leaned back in his chair, and put his hands behind his head. So far, as the youngest son of a well-established, well-to-do business family in the small city of Svensund, his life had been pretty easy.

"I can adjust to whatever I need to," he said. "I can't think of a certain incident—I just take it as it comes and go with the flow—you know what I mean?"

"Okay. And how do you think you'll handle being gone from your family for ten months?"

Henrik wanted to say "No problem," but he knew that wasn't the proper answer.

"I'm sure I'll miss them, but I'll know I'll see them again. It's time for me to be on my own."

"So you think you'll be able to float through this experience without any problems at all?"

"I'd guess so. Which should make it easy on my host family, don't you think?"

"To be honest, I think you might be in for a few surprises if you go," the interviewer said. He looked down at his sheet of questions.

"Do you smoke?"

"No." Henrik knew the organization didn't allow smoking, so there was no point in telling the truth.

The interview continued with a few more questions, and then the interviewer handed Henrik several sheets of paper.

"We ask each applicant to write a personal essay that will be read by potential host families. You may use the computer in the next room, or you may hand write it, whichever you prefer. When you're finished, leave it with the secretary. We'll be in touch."

Henrik unfolded his 6 foot, 3 inch frame and rose from his chair. He reached out and shook the interviewer's hand. "It was a pleasure to meet you, sir," he said, flashing his best smile. "If I have the opportunity to go to the United States, I promise to be a good representative of my country."

"I'm sure you will," the interviewer said. Henrik wondered if he heard a slight touch of sarcasm in the man's voice. Nothing to worry about. If he was supposed to go, he would. If not, it was no skin off his back.

Dear Host Family,

   My name is Henrik Svensson, and I am 17 years old. I live in a small city in northern Sweden called Svensund. The town was named after my great-great-grandfather when he came here and started a lumber business. The business is still in my family today, and it now makes pine furniture out of the lumber we harvest.

   I am the youngest of four in my family. My oldest brother, Marten, is 23 and he is working in the business. My sisters, Catharina and Gabriella, are 21 and 19, and they are in university. My father and mother both work at the business, so you can see it is a family thing. I suppose some-day I will be in the business too.

   I go to gymnasium school in my village—there are 700 people in the school. I ride my bike there. My favorite sub-jects are music, history, and biology. After school I come home, eat, study a bit, and do things with my friends. I like sports and am playing on a soccer team in our village. I have been playing soccer since I was 10, so I guess I am quite good. This year our team has been winning a lot of games. That is a lot of fun. I would like to play soccer in the U.S. too, and maybe go to a university on a soccer scholarship. On summer holidays we go to Spain and there I love to sail and play beach volleyball. I would like to do that in the U.S. too.

   We have two animals in our house—a dog and a cat. The dog's name is Alpha and the cat's name is Busahn. Sometimes I take the dog for walks—that can be a real pain but it has to be done.

You probably wonder why a guy like me would want to leave the most beautiful country in the world to go to the United States for a year. I can say that it is because I want to improve my English, and the United States is a good place to do that. For my new family, I want them to know that I will not be a problem. I know how to act and I have traveled with my father on business trips. I can take care of myself so don't worry about me. See you soon,

Henrik Svensson

Henrik read his essay. He couldn't think of anything else to say. That'll do, he thought. Take it or leave it. He handed it to the secretary at the desk, and walked out the door.

The notification of his acceptance came two weeks later. Unless he contacted the organization to say he wanted to reconsider, Henrik's profile would be sent to the United States, along with hundreds of others, to be viewed by families who were willing to host an exchange student. "Congratulations," the letter said, "We will let you know when you have a family."

Henrik wasn't sure if he was excited or not. It still didn't seem real. But the day he heard about his placement, it began to sink in, and he knew how he felt then. Angry. Slam-the-door-and-yell angry.

On the morning of March 23, Henrik was quickly checking his computer e-mail messages before going to school. One was from the exchange organization. He read it twice, then printed it out and ran down the stairs, across the large living room, and into the kitchen. His parents were having a cup of coffee and quick breakfast before leaving for work.

"You won't believe this," he raged, waving the sheet of paper in front of his father. "Why me?"

"What's the matter, Henrik?" his mother asked, looking up from the newspaper.

"I got my placement. I'm going to Kansas! Kansas, of all the God-forsaken places in the world. What am I supposed to do there? Watch tornadoes?"

"Bo Riggs and Skye Martin. Wellsford, Kansas," Henrik's father read from the sheet. "Occupations: Harley Davidson shop owner and recording artist." He looked up at Henrik. "Now what's so bad about that? Sounds pretty interesting to me."

"Are you kidding? He probably trades used Harley's out of a run-down shack behind his farm house, and she probably sings country music at the local county fair!" Henrik slumped into a chair at the table. "There's nothing in Kansas but flat land and cowboys. I don't think this is such a good idea, Dad. If you want me to improve my English, I don't think Kansas is the place to send me."

Henrik's mother reached over to pick up the sheet. "Here's a phone number and an e-mail address. Why don't you write and find out more about them before you jump to conclusions?"

"And then what? Drop out?"

"Maybe you'll find out it isn't so bad after all."

"Yeah, right."

"Remember, Marten and Gabi and Cathy all had a great time as exchange students."

"Yeah, but they weren't in Kansas."

"No, they were in Iowa, Minnesota, and Georgia. And none of them were in a big city, if that's what you're after."

Henrik glared at his mother in exasperation. "Doesn't it mean anything that you paid a lot of money for me to go? I should at least get the east or west coast. It's easy for you to say it won't be problem. You don't have to live there! I'm the one who'll be out of civilization for ten months. That's a long time to live in Dodge City."

"You aren't going to Dodge City. It says Wellsford, Henrik," his father corrected.

"Dodge City, Wellsford, Cowboyland, Indianville—it's all the same," Henrik spluttered. "I can't wait to tell the kids at school."

They laughed. They joked about how he'd look in cowboy boots, and if they'd be able to understand his English when he came back to Sweden. And his girlfriend Lisa said something that he hadn't thought about—something that worried him even more than the cowboy jokes.

"You know Kansas is in the middle of the Bible belt, don't you?" Lisa asked. "Everybody goes to church and nobody has any fun. You'll have to go to church three times a week at least."

"Who says?" Henrik asked.

"I know somebody that was in Kansas. Her host family made her go to church with them. And they had all kinds of stupid rules."

"Like what?"

"Like times when she had to be home, and she couldn't have her boyfriend in her room, and she couldn't drink or smoke— stuff like that."

Henrik drew Lisa close to him and wrapped his arms around her waist.

"Well, they won't have to worry about me having a *boyfriend* in my room. As far as smoking and drinking, you can't tell me the host parents are watching all the time. I'll figure something out."

"I was hoping to visit you in California, but now that you're going to Kansas...." Lisa let her voice trail off.

"There's still hope. My parents are going to talk to the organization and try to get my placement changed."

"Good," Lisa smiled.

The news from Henrik's parents that evening was not good. The interviewer had told them that Henrik had "an attitude." He'd only been accepted into the program because his parents carried a lot of influence, his siblings had been successful students, and he "hoped a year in the U.S. would help the kid grow up."

Grow up. Henrik snorted at the words his mother repeated. It was obvious who had the attitude problem—that snippy little interviewer. He'd probably sent Henrik to Kansas just out of spite.

TWO

SPRING comes softly to northern Sweden, and never soon enough. The dark, cold days of the long winter seem endless, and a person's sanity is saved only by the certainty that the sun will return in the course of the seasons and will shine for long luxurious days through the short summer. Winters are for sleeping and working in northern Sweden. Summers are for staying up with the sun, taking vacations, and celebrating the beauty of a creation gone green.

Mid-Summer is the highlight of the season. The arrival of the summer solstice and the longest day, when darkness never invades the nighttime hours, signifies that life is coming full circle. It is a time to celebrate with flowers, dancing, drinking, feasting and frolicking. It is the best day of the year.

Henrik had always looked forward to Mid-Summer, but this year he enjoyed it more than he ever had before. It would probably be his last real reason to celebrate anything until he returned to Sweden next year. Even his friends, none of whom ever turned down a chance to party, commented on his boisterous behavior.

"No matter how much you put down, you can't stay drunk for an entire year," his buddy, Lars, kidded. "Face it Henrik, you're going to Kansas!"

Actually, Henrik was beginning to think living with Bo and Skye, his host parents, wouldn't be so bad after all. He'd learned more about them from their e-mails, and they'd sent a picture of the two of them sitting on the front steps of a log house with a black and white dog between them. Definitely better than an old white farm house. Bo apparently had a legitimate Harley David-son shop in the city of Vicksburg. Having a city within driving distance gave Henrik some hope of having someplace to go and something to do.

And Skye was more than just a small-town singer. The CD's she'd sent were pretty good, especially the older ones. Her last one was mostly Christian rock stuff, which didn't do much for him, but at least it was rock, and not country music. Yeah, he could probably survive a year with Bo and Skye.

The big unknown was the school. He'd be attending "a large high school in the middle of nowhere," Skye had written. Appar-ently it was an attendance center for kids from a large rural area. Henrik figured it was the only way they could have enough kids to make a school.

Rolling Prairie High School. The name certainly fit his men-tal pictures of Kansas. Three hundred students stuck in the middle of the prairie, where there was probably nothing to do but study.

Then there was the matter of getting to school. Public trans-portation was virtually non-existent, biking was impractical, and the exchange organization didn't allow students to drive. Besides, he wouldn't have his Swedish driver's license until he was 18. So how was he going to get to school and back, he asked in one of his e-mails to Skye and Bo.

"We have a horse," Bo answered. "He's fast, and on a good day it should only take you 30 minutes to get to school. Provid-ing, of course, you stay on him. He has been known to lose peo-ple along the way." Henrik couldn't believe what he was reading. "Of course, if you don't like that option, one of us will take you to school. There are also some neighbor kids around that might be willing to give you a ride. We'll work something out."

Henrik smiled. So, Bo had a sense of humor. That would be helpful.

"What, really, will you get out of being an exchange student for a year?" Lars asked one night in mid-July. It was 2:00 a.m. and he and Henrik were on the Svensson patio, drinking a beer after biking home from a soccer game in the early morning light. It was hard going to bed while it was still light, so they often didn't. They could sleep in the winter. Summer was a time for hanging out and making the most of the long days.

"What will I get out of the year? Women, mostly," Henrik chuckled, taking a drink from his bottle. "They can't be hard to catch in Kansas. Surely a suave, sophisticated Swedish dude could pick up a few women, don't you think?"

"No problem. Love 'em and leave 'em. It could be a great ten months. Just don't fall in love or anything stupid like that."

"Not a chance. They're probably all bow-legged, flat-chested farm girls."

Lars laughed, nearly choking on his beer. The two guys spent the next few minutes listing the potential favorable and unfavorable qualities of Kansas girls. The conversation grew cruder as the minutes went by and the beer went down. Around 3:00 a.m., they watched the sun come up and then fell asleep on the patio.

A pesky fly finally forced Henrik awake around 8:00 that morning. He sat up, groaned, and laid back down. He hated mornings like this. Even more, he hated that he was supposed to be at work at 8:00. Henrik vaguely remembered his father nudging him some time ago, then muttering something under his breath. He'd heard the Volvo back out of the driveway before he'd fallen back asleep. Now he had to get up, shower, and go to work.

Lars was still asleep on the chaise lounge next to him. He didn't have a job this summer, lucky guy.

There were advantages as well as disadvantages of being in a family-owned business. There was always a summer job for the kids, but there was never a choice between working and not working. His father would not allow his children a free ride. He insisted they earn their spending money, and they would do it in the family lumber and furniture business.

Henrik walked slowly toward the large, square white house. His friends called it "The White House", because it reminded them of the elegant building where the President of the United States lived. It didn't seem elegant to Henrik—it was just home. Sure, it had a lot of rooms, and he had his own space with a sleeping area, TV room, and bathroom. Some of his friends said he was spoiled, but he knew better. Spoiled kids didn't have to work. He groaned, hoping a shower would help him feel better.

An hour later, Henrik was sitting on the floor at the furniture factory, sanding one of the legs on a dining room table. This summer, his father had given him the job of building several pieces of furniture. "You need to feel the wood, work it, get to know it," his father explained. "If you are going to sell our pieces someday, you need to know them inside and out."

Henrik had already spent a year learning about the lumber business, going out with the men who tagged and harvested the trees. He knew how to select a tree that would make a nice piece of furniture. But he still had a lot to learn, in his father's opinion. Personally, Henrik felt he needed a break from learning about furniture. He'd never thought of the exchange program as a means of escape, but the more time he spent in the furniture factory that summer, the more he realized what a great opportunity it was. A whole year without his parents trying to guide him into the business. A year of easy school work, American girls, fast food, and whatever else he could find.

"So, you finally made it to work?" his father's voice broke into Henrik's thoughts. Henrik grunted and kept his eyes on the table leg he was sanding.

"You're lucky. Other employers wouldn't put up with you coming to work late half the time." Henrik looked straight ahead and watched his father's trouser leg come closer. "You're doing a pretty good job on this," his father said, running his hand across the table. "You know wood, and you have a nice touch. Now if we could just get the rest of you to grow up." Henrik stopped sanding. One more comment...

"Personally, I'm glad you're going to Kansas. It's good for you not to always get what you want."

Henrik stood up and stared into the steel blue eyes that mirrored his own. He was tall, but still an inch shorter than his father. Years of work in the lumber business as a young man had broadened the older man's shoulders, and his life-long love of sports kept him trim.

"Lucky. You say I'm lucky to be able to work here in this business. This fine family business." Henrik punched out his words with such force that it almost seemed as if he was physically striking the man in front of him. "Well maybe I don't feel so lucky. Maybe I don't want to be like everybody else in this family. Maybe I want to be a bum and play beach volleyball in California for the rest of my life. You say I always get what I want. Hardly. If I did, I wouldn't be working here and I wouldn't be an exchange student. I'd be doing what I want to do, not what I'm expected to do. But NO! I come to work while my friends sleep in, and I go to Kansas to grow up. Just don't call me lucky and don't talk to me about always getting what I want, because it ain't true!"

Henrik's father displayed no emotion during his son's verbal attack. When Henrik was finished, he simply looked at him and said, "When you turn 18, Henrik, you are on your own." Then he turned and walked away.

THREE

THE SUBJECT never came up again. Henrik worked two more weeks, then spent his last week in Sweden partying with his friends and making preparations to leave. Saying good-bye to his family before boarding the plane in Stockholm had been no big deal. He'd hugged his mother and sisters, shaken hands with his father and brother, and walked onto the plane.

Parting with his girlfriend, Lisa, had been more difficult. She was going to England for a few months to study, and they had decided to break up before each of them left Sweden, since they both wanted to be free to meet and date new people. Henrik was glad Lisa had agreed, because the pursuit of American girls was definitely part of his plan.

There were other exchange students on the flight, and Henrik compared notes with two that were also going to Kansas. One of them, a heavy-set kid named Andreas Carlson, was going to stay with a family in Vicksburg, the city where their plane would land, and where Bo had his motorcycle shop. Andreas seemed nice enough, but with that extra weight he carried around, he might have a hard time getting women to like him, Henrik thought, smirking to himself. Thank goodness that was one problem he didn't have to worry about.

Henrik had been awake for 24 hours when the plane landed at Vicksburg. As they taxied to the terminal, the captain came on the loudspeaker and welcomed them to Vicksburg. "The local time is 5:20 p.m. and the temperature is 98 degrees. If you are visiting, we hope you enjoy your stay in Vicksburg, and if you live here, welcome home!"

Henrik looked at his watch: 17:20 Swedish time. And 98 degrees? He wasn't sure exactly what that translated to in Celsius, but he knew it was very hot. When the plane stopped, he stood up and reached for his bag in the overhead compartment.

"Well, this is it," he heard Andreas say behind him.

"It's about time," Henrik said. "I've been on planes long enough."

"Are you scared?"

"Scared? About what?"

"You know. Meeting the family. What if you don't like them?"

"If I don't like them, I'll get a new family. The organization promised that."

"I guess so. I think it's just hitting me now."

"Well there's no turning back, my friend." Henrik slapped Andreas on the shoulder. "Let's go."

They joined the line of passengers leaving the plane, then walked down the ramp and into the lounge area.

Henrik saw them right away. They looked just like their picture. Bo was tall and lean, dressed in black jeans and a black Harley-Davidson T-shirt. Skye stood next to him, her deeply tanned arms and legs a striking contrast to her white shorts and shirt. They were both wearing big smiles, and Skye was holding a helium-filled balloon that proclaimed, "It's a boy!"

"Hello, Henrik," Bo said, in the deepest voice Henrik had ever heard. He shook Bo's outstretched hand. "Hi, Bo, Skye." He turned to Skye, who gave him a big hug.

"Welcome to Kansas," Skye said. Then she giggled. "Sorry about the silly balloon. We don't have any children, and some friends gave it to us and insisted we bring it to the airport."

"It's okay," Henrik said. It was kind of silly. "As long as I don't have to sleep in a baby bed."

Bo's laugh was loud and deep. "No problem!"'

"I bet you're really tired," Skye said. Henrik noticed her green eyes when she looked up him.

"Sort of," he said. "Where do we get our baggage?"

"This way." Bo led the way down the wide terminal hall. "Hope it all got here okay."

"It better," Henrik said.

He had never known heat like this. Not even in Spain, where his family spent their vacations enjoying the sun and sea. He might have stepped into an oven, or into hell itself, Henrik thought as he stood on the sidewalk outside the airport terminal. He and Skye were waiting for Bo to bring the pickup from the parking lot. All of his luggage had arrived safely. Poor Andreas. His was lost somewhere between Stockholm and Vicksburg.

"Sorry about the heat. I guess you're not used to this, are you?" Skye remarked, pushing her long blond hair behind her ears.

"Not really. How long will it be like this?"

"Oh, a couple more weeks and it'll start cooling off."

A couple of weeks. He could be dead by then.

"I tried to get a placement in California," he said. "I suppose it's hot there, too, but they have the ocean."

"Yeah, I guess you're stuck with us in Kansas," Skye remarked.

Bo pulled up in a new-looking dark green pickup truck. He jumped out and grabbed one of Henrik's suitcases. "We can put one in the club cab with you, and the other in the back," Bo said. "Do you have anything in either one that shouldn't be in the heat?"

"Just some chocolate, but I don't know which one it's in,"

Henrik answered.

"Well we could put both suitcases in the cab and you could ride in the back."

"Yeah, right!" Henrik said. Then he realized Bo was joking, but he didn't think it was very funny.

"I think the chocolate's in that one," Henrik pointed to the large black suitcase, and watched as Bo picked it up and sandwiched it into the back seat. Henrik lifted the other suitcase into the bed of the truck, then climbed in next to the black suitcase. Not very comfortable for a tall guy, he thought.

"You okay back there?" Skye asked, leaning around from her front seat. "I could trade places with you."

"I'll be all right," Henrik said. When I get back to Sweden, he thought.

The ride from Vicksburg lasted an eternity. They asked if he was hungry. No, he wasn't. Not even for a burger from McDonalds? No. They asked if it was hard to leave his family. No, it wasn't. They asked if he'd left a girlfriend in Sweden. No, he hadn't. Oh, then he was a free man, huh? Yes, he was. They asked if he was going out for football. He didn't know. He didn't know if he'd live through this heat, much less play sports in it. They said he'd make a great kicker for the team, since he played soccer, and that sports were a good way to get involved in the school. Yeah. They said they'd have some members of the football team at their place tomorrow to meet him. Sure.

The countryside was incredibly flat, open, and boring. A few trees, but mostly fields and pastures. Heat haze hung over everything. If he hadn't been riding in an air-conditioned vehicle, he would have passed out, he knew for sure.

"Is your house air-conditioned?" he asked.

"You bet it is," Bo answered. "And the school is too." Then he turned to Skye and said, "What do you think, honey? Shall we wait awhile before we take him to visit your grandparents?"

"At least until he's used to the heat," she agreed. Turning to look at Henrik, she said, "My grandparents are Amish. They don't have air-conditioned homes. They don't even have electricity."

"Or cars, or phones, or any of that modern stuff," Bo added.

"So what's up with them?" Henrik wondered.

"It's part of their religion. They don't believe in having worldly things."

So, Skye's grandparents were in some kind of conservative cult. Skye and Bo thought he should kill himself playing football in this heat. He'd spend ten months going places cramped in the seat of their club cab pickup like a little kid. This was going to be a great year.

Bo slowed the pickup and turned into a long lane that led back to what seemed to be the middle of a cow pasture. Then Henrik recognized the log house he'd seen in the picture, and on the porch, the black and white dog. Bo stopped the truck and got out. The dog ran up to him, carrying a stick in its mouth.

"Hey, Zeb buddy," Bo said. "No, I don't want to play stick right now. Go say Hi to Henrik."

Henrik eased his way out of the air-conditioned truck and into the heat. He looked down at the dog, who was looking up at him with bright, alert eyes and a stick in its mouth.

"His name is Zeb. He's a Border Collie, and he loves to retrieve sticks that people throw," Skye explained.

"Obviously," Henrik said. "How'd he know to come to me when Bo said 'Go to Henrik'?"

"Incredibly intelligent dog," Bo said, grunting as he lifted the suitcase out of the cab.

"No, he'll just try anybody until he finds someone who'll play with him," Skye countered.

"Like I said, incredibly intelligent dog."

Henrik lifted the suitcase from the back of the truck and followed Bo and Skye to the house. Zeb trailed behind them. Skye opened the front door and they stepped inside. From lifelong habit, Henrik slipped off his shoes and left them near the door. The house wasn't large, but it was nice, he thought as he looked around. He could see most of the main floor. Lots of wood and windows. On the left was the kitchen; in front of him, a pine dining table. The family room with couch, entertainment center and large windows was to his right.

"Welcome home," Skye said. "It's nothing fancy, but hey, it's cool."

That it was. Thank goodness their house had air-conditioning.

"Your room is right over here," Skye continued. She walked across the dining area, opened a door and switched on the light.

"Hope you don't mind—it has kind of a Harley theme," she said, smiling at Henrik. No kidding. A Harley-Davidson bedspread, curtains, and wastebasket. A huge Harley poster on the wall. The room was about half the size of his at home.

"We have our own bathroom upstairs, so this one down here is pretty much yours," Skye said, walking to a nearby door. She flipped on the light and Henrik looked in. Strange—he'd never seen carpet in a bathroom before. "Would you like to see the rest of the place now, or do you want to get some sleep?" Skye asked. "You must be feeling like a zombie by now."

She was right about that. All he wanted was a shower and bed.

Henrik sat on the bed after his shower, staring at his open suitcases and taking stock of situation. He's guessed wrong about the chocolate. It had melted into a gooey mess, but Skye had assured him that a night in the freezer would do wonders for it. She'd seemed thrilled with the handwoven rug his mother had sent for her, and Bo said he liked his beer stein. They were nice enough people. It's just that they lived in a pasture, in Kansas, in heat that nearly made him sick. They wanted him to play foot-ball. Did that mean they were going to make demands on him like his parents? That's what he wanted to get away from. He fell back against the pillow, pulled the sheet around him, and closed his eyes. He was too tired to think about it now.

He dreamed he was being stuffed into a pickup truck with Andreas. The fat boy was sweating and crying. The heat was unbearable, and they couldn't get the windows down. They both began screaming and pounding against the window. Andreas was yelling in English, "HELP! HELP! HELP!"

Henrik woke with a start. The screams were real! It was night and the screams were coming from outside his window.

FOUR

"WE TRIED to warn you about the peacocks," Skye smiled sympathetically at Henrik the next morning. "But I know—no amount of warning prepares you for the sound when you hear it. Especially when it wakes you up from a sound sleep. I'm really sorry."

"It's no big deal," Henrik said between bites of his breakfast sandwich. "Just scared me to death, that's all."

"I understand, but I'm not sure what we can do," Skye looked helplessly at Bo.

"Me neither," Bo replied, grinning at Henrik across the table. "I haven't seen any peacock muzzles in the Wellsford Hardware store, but I do recall seeing some earplugs that might fit Henrik. Or we could go out and explain to the birds what a pain they are, and ask if they could please respect Henrik's sleeping rights."

Henrik stared at Bo. Was he making fun of him? If so, he'd call the organization right now and ask to be moved. He hadn't paid $5,000 to sleep next to screaming peacocks and have his host father laugh at him about it.

"Come on, Henrik, let me show you around," Bo stood up from the table. "You should see the screaming birds—they really are pretty. And I'm sure Zeb is ready to play stick with you."

He could hardly wait. The great Kansas farm tour. He should be in California heading for the beach to play volleyball. Instead he was going to look at big noisy birds and play with a dog and a stick. How unlucky could a guy get?

The worst part of being stuck in Kansas wasn't living on a farm. The worst part was the heat and humidity. When Henrik stepped outside at 9:00 a.m., the thermometer by the back door read 86 degrees Fahrenheit . Henrik looked at the smaller Centigrade numbers. Thirty degrees.

"It's going to be another hot one," Bo said, reaching down to greet Zeb. "You can see why they have football practice at 5:30 in the morning."

"Who has football practice at 5:30?"

"The high school. It starts on Monday. Are you going out?"

"I don't know."

Henrik followed Bo and Zeb across the yard toward a new, rust-red building. Although not as large, it looked like some of the barns Henrik had seen on their way home from Vicksburg yesterday. Bo opened a gate in the white fence next to the barn and walked through with Zeb close beside him. The Border Collie immediately pricked up his ears and stared at something in the distance.

"What's he see?" Henrik asked, entering the enclosure.

Bo closed and latched the gate before answering. "The sheep are out there in the pasture, and Zeb's a sheep dog. Some of them are wearing bells, and he hears them. If I give him the signal, he'll bring the herd home."

"Really." Henrik was vaguely intrigued. So, the dog did more than play with sticks.

"Really," Bo repeated. "I'd show you now, but the sheep need to graze before it gets too hot, and there's no need to make them run in and then go back out again. But you'll see Zeb work them sometime."

Zeb looked up at Bo, and then back in the direction of the sheep. Henrik picked up a stick. "Here, Zeb," he said, wondering if the dog could be distracted with his favorite pastime.

Zeb looked at Henrik and the stick, then back at Bo before returning his attention to the sheep.

"He knows his job, and he knows his toy. He knows the minute he steps through that gate he's on the job," Bo explained.

"Good for him."

Bo stepped into the barn and returned with a can of grain which he scattered the on the ground. Moments later two peacocks and half a dozen funny-looking gray birds had arrived and were pecking at the grain.

"This would be your opportunity to discuss the screaming with these fellows," said Bo, indicating the big birds with the bright blue heads and chests.

"Like they'll listen to me," Henrik muttered. "What are the gray birds?"

"Guineas. They're good for eating mosquitoes, bugs and ticks. And they make a loud obnoxious noise, too."

Henrik slapped his arm. Speaking of mosquitoes . . .

"We aren't really farmers," Bo continued. "We just keep a few animals around for the fun of it, and the sheep keep the pasture mowed. We have a llama, too. He protects the sheep from coyotes. You'll see him when the sheep come home."

I can hardly wait, Henrik thought.

He spent the rest of the day unpacking, sending e-mails home to family and friends, watching TV and just hanging out. He stayed inside. The heat made him sick.

Before he left Sweden Skye had warned him in one of her e-mails that they went to church on Sunday morning, and that as part of their family, he would be expected to go with them. It was just another thing he'd have to tolerate. The next day was Sunday. He'd hoped for some leniency, since he was still getting used to the time change, but Skye woke him at 8:00 and said they'd be leaving for church in an hour.

Wellsford Mennonite Church, a simple, red brick building near the center of the town, looked nothing like the churches Henrik had seen in Sweden. Inside, the differences were even greater. There were no pictures, or statues, or altars, or anything of a religious nature in the Mennonite church. It was so plain, Henrik thought in surprise. Plain pews, plain windows, a plain podium at the front.

They were greeted by smiling, friendly people of all ages who seemed happy to be in church and delighted to meet him. Strange, he thought. At home, church was for old people, or for those who were being confirmed, or getting married, or who had died. Most of the people Henrik knew only attended church on Christmas and Easter.

A tall, slender, dark-haired girl about his age ushered them to a pew near the front of the church.

"Her name is Mattie," Skye whispered to him when they were seated. "She's a senior at your high school, and she's in the youth group you'll be joining."

"Okay," he replied. Pretty girl. He bet she was a—

"And she lives near us, so maybe she'll be willing to take you places," Skye continued. Okay, if he had to be chauffeured around Kansas by a pretty church-going girl, then so be it. When it came to girls, he'd always liked a challenge.

From the beginning, the service was different from anything he'd ever experienced. He wasn't thrilled about being publicly introduced to the entire congregation, but he smiled and waved anyway. He didn't know any of the songs, but they were livelier than the ones he remembered from the few times he'd attended church in Sweden. The pastor was a woman named Marge Enninger. At home, the few times he'd been in church, a man wearing some kind of robe had been in charge of the service.

This woman was in her 50's, with a soft, clear voice and short brown hair flecked with gray. When she delivered her sermon, it was more like a conversation with the congregation, rather than preaching. Henrik didn't pay much attention to what she said—partly because he was still getting used to hearing so much English being spoken so fast, and partly because he figured it wouldn't be interesting to him.

He sighed thankfully when they stood up for the last song at the close of the service an hour later. Not exactly pleasant, but not life threatening, either. He figured he could tolerate it once a week. Ten months . . . that would be 40 church services! Oh well, one down, 39 to go.

But there was more. Something called Sunday school. Skye showed him to a room where about a dozen kids his age sat around a table. "Ray, this is our exchange student, Henrik Svensson," she introduced him to an older man who was obviously the teacher. "Henrik, this is Ray Fry, and this is the high school Sunday school class. Have fun!" she told him as she left the room.

Henrik pulled out a chair at the end of the table and sat down.

"Welcome, Henrik," Ray said. "We'll go around and say our names. We won't expect you to remember them right away, but I bet you'll know them soon. Any guy smart enough to be an exchange student is probably smart enough to learn names pretty fast."

"I don't know about that," Henrik said. *Don't mess with me,* he thought. After they'd introduced themselves, he could only remember two names: Mattie, the girl who had ushered them into the church, and Winston. Any guy with a cigarette for a name should be interesting, he thought. Winston didn't look like the perfect little Mennonite boy. He wondered if Winston-boy could help him get some Winston-cigs. Ray-the-teacher tried to involve him in the class discussion, but Henrik pleaded innocence, saying he was just there to listen. That seemed to please Ray, and it got Henrik off the hook. There were also 39 more hours of Sunday school, he thought, just as a buzzer rang to let them know class was finally over.

"You going to Rolling Prairie High School?" Winston asked as they filed out of the room.

"Yeah. You go there?"

"Everybody here goes there," Winston grinned. "You coming out for football?"

"I don't know. You play?" Winston was shorter and heavier than Henrik. He looked strong.

"Yeah. You oughta come out. Do you play soccer? We could use a kicker."

"I'll see. Practice starts tomorrow?"

"5:30 a.m."

"That's an ungodly time to be up playing football."

"Beats dying in the heat."

"I suppose. Well, I'll see."

"Either way, I guess I'll see you in school tomorrow," Winston said. They'd reached the front door of the church, and Bo and Skye were there, talking to Pastor Marge.

"So this is the new member of your family," Marge said, extending her hand to Henrik. Her handshake was strong and firm. "We're glad to have you here. I'm Marge Enninger."

"Henrik Svennson. Nice to meet you."

"What part of Sweden are you from, Henrik?"

"The north."

"How far north? Like, how far are you from Ostersund?" Marge's intense brown eyes studied Henrik.

"Ostersund? Have you been there?"

"Yes. My sister and her husband hosted a student from there. When they went to Sweden to visit her, I went along."

"I'm from Svensund, about an hour north of Ostersund."

"Beautiful country up there. I would love to go back," Marge said.

"Yes, it is beautiful," Henrik said. "The summers are great."

"I'll never forget the time we spent there that summer. It never did get dark at night, and the weather was just perfect. I bet this Kansas heat is nearly driving you crazy," Marge said.

"Yeah," Henrik said, finally feeling like someone understood him. She'd been there.

"Did you bring pictures along? I'd love to see them sometime. And I'll show you mine," Marge said.

"What are you doing this evening?" Skye asked "Why don't you come over for supper and bring your pictures?"

"It's a date," Marge said, looking up at Henrik. "Is that okay with you?"

"Fine with me," he said. He couldn't say what he thought: *No thanks, Pastor Marge, I'd rather watch a movie than look at your vacation pictures.*

"Maybe we'll have Dawdi and Grandma over too," Skye said. "They love to look at pictures, and they want to meet Henrik."

It was settled. Henrik would spend his first Sunday evening in America with his host parents, a Mennonite pastor, and an old Amish couple. It had to be the most uncool, potentially boring thing a guy could do.

FIVE

HENRIK spent the afternoon in the family room watching a football game on TV. Halfway through the fourth quarter, he heard Zeb barking outside. There was another sound, like a rattle, that Henrik couldn't identify. He got up from the couch and walked over to the window. A horse-drawn buggy was coming down the drive. It was open—like a convertible car, he guessed—and as it passed by the window, he saw an elderly couple seated inside. The buggy stopped next to the barn in front of two wooden posts supporting a crossbar. Henrik had wondered what it was for, but hadn't asked Bo.

The old man stepped down from the buggy, and tied the horse to the wooden crossbar. Then he walked around to the other side to help the old woman climb down, but she was too quick for him. She stood next to the buggy and waited while he reached behind the wooden seat and lifted out a picnic basket.

Henrik studied the couple as they approached the house. The man was about average in height and weight, and walked with a slight limp. He was wearing a light blue shirt and dark navy pants held up with suspenders. A straw hat covered his head, and a long gray beard spread from his face down across his chest.

The petite, elderly woman wore a long, dark green dress and a stiff black bonnet. Henrik thought she looked like she'd just stepped off the set of a western movie. He couldn't imagine why anyone would choose to wear such clothes in this awful heat. Skye was standing at the door, waiting to invite her grandparents in. Henrik turned from the window as they entered the house.

"Hello, Dawdi and Grandma," Skye greeted them. "Come in where it's cool!"

"Don't mind if we do," Dawdi said, taking off his hat and setting it on a chair near the door. "It's a warm one today, that's for sure."

Grandma took off her heavy black bonnet. Her white hair was pulled back from her face and hidden under a lightweight white bonnet. Did these people have a thing about covering their heads or what, Henrik thought.

"How nice of you to have us over, Skye," Grandma said. "I brought a pie for dessert, and some diabetic brownies for you. I hope you don't mind."

"Mind! Grandma, you know Bo loves your pies!" Skye exclaimed. "And I'm sure Henrik will too, once he's tried a piece."

Dawdi was looking at Henrik, and he knew it was time for introductions. He walked over to the old gentleman and stuck out his hand. "Henrik Svensson," he said.

"Jonas Bontrager," the man replied. "Pleased to meet you. And this is my wife, Sue Ann."

Henrik reached down to shake the hand of the woman standing in front of him. She grasped his large hand in both of her small ones and looked up at him with the brightest brown eyes he'd ever seen in a woman that age. Actually, he realized, he didn't know very many elderly people. "I am so happy to meet you, Henrik," she said, smiling. "Finally, Skye gives me a great-grandson!"

"That's right, Grandma, and you don't even have to change the diapers on this one," Skye teased.

Dawdi laughed, a slow, comfortable old-man laugh. "It's a

good thing, I'm thinking. They would surely be big diapers."

Henrik laughed out loud in spite of himself. This Dawdi—what kind of man was he? Conservative, Amish and, according to Skye, a minister in the church. Henrik had expected a stuffy old man, not one who'd joke about him wearing diapers.

Pastor Marge arrived soon after Dawdi and Grandma, and they sat down to grilled hamburgers, salad, watermelon, and corn on the cob. The meal was delicious, Henrik had to admit, filling his plate with everything a second time. He let the conversation flow around him, speaking only when someone asked him a question.

"Henrik, do you want some of Grandma's best-in-the-world pie now, or would you prefer to wait until after we look at the pictures?" Skye asked when everyone had emptied their plates.

"Doesn't matter to me," he answered. "Whatever you want."

"It matters to me," Bo rumbled. "I don't have an inch of space left inside for pie right now. I say we wait."

"Sounds good to me," Marge chimed in. "I'm going to have to pretend I'm walking through the scenes in the pictures, getting some exercise, so I have room for pie later."

"Does that really work, Marge?" Skye teased. "Because if it does, I could save myself lots of miles of power walking."

"Now don't you stop that walking," Grandma admonished. "We look for you every morning. We'd miss you if you didn't walk past our place."

"Don't worry, Grandma, I'm addicted. I'll be walking forever."

"Well, I hear the couch calling me now," Bo stood up. "I think it's time for the men to retreat to the family room while the women clean the table. Isn't that the way they do it in Sweden, Henrik?"

"Sure," Henrik agreed, noticing the look that passed between Bo and Skye. Bo had a silly grin on his face, and Skye seemed slightly disgusted.

"Don't let him pollute your mind," Skye told Henrik. "He will take every opportunity to do that, and you have to be careful."

"She's right, you know," Dawdi added. "Bo will have you believing that not only should men stay out of the kitchen, but women should stay off motorcycles." His blue eyes danced. He was clearly enjoying this bit of conversation. "And Skye will be the first to straighten him out. If you want my opinion, son," Dawdi grew quiet and leaned toward Henrik to whisper, "If you want my opinion, don't mess with Skye. Bo may look tough, but he's a pushover. It's Skye you have to watch out for. I should know. I've known her all her life, and I could tell you some stories.

"I'd like to hear some," Henrik said. "I might need them sometime. You know, blackmail material." He found himself warming up to this Dawdi man.

"Another time, then. Come over. We'll have some tea and cookies, and talk."

"I'll do that," Henrik said.

He went to his room and picked up the photos he'd brought from Sweden.

There weren't many. He wouldn't have brought them at all if his mother hadn't insisted. Whether he cared or not, she knew his host family would want to see pictures of his home and family. Marge, on the other hand, had a pile of scrapbooks and even a video.

The men talked while the women cleared the table, and then they joined the men in the family room.

"I brought my video along but, Jonas and Sue Ann, I respect the fact that you don't watch television. So we don't have to look at it—there are lots of pictures of the same places."

Henrik noticed Grandma and Dawdi, seated next to each other on the couch, exchange glances.

"I think it will be okay," Dawdi said. "It is a clean movie, isn't it?"

"It sure is, Jonas. Sweden is one of the cleanest countries I've ever seen. Everything is neat and tidy," Marge answered. "That is what you meant, isn't it?"

"Yes, of course," Dawdi's eyes twinkled.

"I think we should start with Henrik, because I could take all evening, and you'd all fall asleep and then you'd never see his pictures," Marge stated, sitting down on a chair near the couch. "So, take it away, Henrik!"

He spread his photographs on the coffee table. "Bo and Skye had some pictures of me and my family before I came, so I didn't bring a lot," he said. "These are my parents—they own a lumber and furniture business that's been in our family for generations. This is our family last Christmas—my brother, Marten, and sisters, Gabriella and Catharina."

"Beautiful girls," Marge said. "Are they still in school?"

"Yes, they're both in the university."

"What are they studying?"

"I don't know for sure—I think economics or business or something. They will probably end up in the family business. Marten is working there already."

"And you? Is that where you will end up too?" Marge asked.

"Not if I can help it."

"No? What would you rather do?" Bo asked.

"Be a bum. Chase women." The answer was out of his mouth before he thought about his audience—a Mennonite pastor, Amish minister, an old Amish woman, and the host parents who would be ruling his life for the next ten months.

"Interesting vocation," Bo broke the brief, uncomfortable silence. "And this picture? Is this a woman you chased and caught?"

It was a picture of Lisa. He wasn't even sure why he'd brought it. "I guess so."

"What's her name?"

"Lisa."

"Is she your girlfriend?" Skye wanted to know.

"She was. We broke up before I left. This is our house, and our dog, Alpha," he pointed to another picture.

"What a beautiful, big house!" Grandma remarked. "To me, it looks kind of like the White House in Washington, D.C."

"Yeah, my friends call it that," he acknowledged. The few pictures remaining were of his soccer team, the family cat, friends, and his family on vacation in Spain.

"Did you bring a camera to take pictures here?" Marge asked.

"Yeah, sure," Henrik answered.

"Good, then you'll have photo albums like mine to show your family when you go home," Marge bubbled.

Not likely, he thought. Marge apparently enjoyed photography, and her photo albums were filled with pictures of Sweden's beautiful scenery. There was certainly nothing scenic about Kansas, and he'd never been big on taking pictures. He'd probably go home with the same number of photos as he'd brought to America. He couldn't say that, of course. What he did say was, "I probably won't have everything organized like you do."

And without a doubt, he wouldn't. Marge's albums were much more than just a group of pictures. They were also diaries and scrapbooks of memorabilia from her trip. If she described everything in those books, it was going to be a long, long evening.

And it was. Sure, Henrik appreciated seeing pictures of his home country. But he didn't know the people, and pictures of someone else's vacations were always boring, no matter where they were taken. He recognized some of the places around Ostersund, including the horse race track. He'd been there a few times.

"You have harness racing in Sweden?" Dawdi asked, peering closely at the pictures.

"Yeah. We have a track in Ostersund," Henrik answered.

"Have you been there?"

"Sure."

"I have some video from the horse races," Marge injected. "Would you like to see it?"

"Yes!" Skye answered immediately.

They had to wait awhile for Marge to run the tape forward and find the right footage. When the harness races appeared on the television screen, Henrik noticed Dawdi leaning closer to the set. He didn't say much, but he studied the scenes flashing before him with obvious interest.

"Dawdi had a race horse once," Skye said. "When my mother was a little girl. Tell them about Preacher, Dawdi."

"Ah, that was a long time ago," Dawdi said, still watching the television intently. "A long time ago, and a long story."

"He won some races, didn't he?" Skye pushed.

"Yah. Yah, he did."

"Did you make a lot of money with him?" Bo wondered.

Dawdi leaned back, and his blue eyes left the screen. "No, I didn't. I sold him."

"Sold him? Why?" It was Marge's turn to be interested.

"Because the church wanted me to," Dawdi said simply.

The room grew quiet except for the voice of the racetrack announcer on the video. Henrik thought surely someone would ask the obvious questions, but no one did, and he wasn't going to. Why, for heaven's sakes, would the church want Dawdi to sell his horse? Ludicrous, Henrik thought. What business did the church have, telling a man what to do with his horse? And if it did, why would a man listen? Maybe this Dawdi wasn't so cool after all. Maybe he was a little off his rocker. Henrik laughed to himself. Yeah, the old man must be off his rocker.

SIX

"WHAT time shall I stand up tomorrow?" Henrik asked Bo and Skye after the Bontragers and Pastor Marge left that evening.

"That's a different way to say it!" Skye laughed. "How long will it take you to get ready? We should leave here by 7:15 to give us time to enroll you before classes start at 8:00."

"So, you're not going to football practice at 5:30?" Bo sounded disappointed.

"Even if he wants to go out for football, he needs to have a physical first," Skye said. "Do you want me to make an appointment with the doctor?"

Henrik had thought about the football thing ever since meeting Winston at church that morning. He hated the idea of playing in the heat. On the other hand, it was a way to meet the guys. He'd need some friends if he were going to survive the next ten months. Especially friends who could help him have a good time. He was anxious to find out if Winston could get him some cigarettes and maybe some beer.

"Yeah, go ahead," he told Skye. "I'll give it a try. Maybe if I just kick, I won't have to do the whole workout."

"Don't count on it," Bo chuckled. "I'm betting you'll have to do it all. Football practice will make a man out of you."

"Did you play?"

"No, he became a man on a Harley," Skye said, grinning at Bo.

"I did, too, play football," Bo said defensively. "Meanest tailback in the league. I can't believe you didn't hear about me back in Pennsylvania."

"Oh, excuse me. It's probably because I didn't follow sports that much when I was in high school."

"I know, you were too busy being the local music sensation," Bo said.

Turning to Henrik, he added, "Skye and her twin sister, Angela, were the hottest number around when they were girls. Everybody knew about the Martin twins, and what talented singers they were."

Henrik didn't know Skye had a twin sister. "So where does Angela live now?"

Skye and Bo looked at each other, then Skye answered softly, "Angela died two years ago. She donated her kidney to me, but she didn't live through the surgery."

"Oh. I'm sorry." Henrik felt uncomfortable. Death wasn't something he was used to talking, or even thinking, about.

"It's okay," Skye replied. "I don't mind talking about Angela. Some day I'll show you my photo albums and tell you all about her. Come to think of it, I guess Angela is partly responsible for you being with us."

Henrik's blue eyes were full of questions.

"She's right," Bo agreed. "Skye made some big changes in her life after Angela died. She quit touring, quit drinking, quit the drugs, married me, settled down, and now here you are."

"I decided I'd rather have God in my life than those things that didn't give me real happiness," Skye added. "Angela was such a good Christian, but I was too busy doing my own thing to think much about God, or anyone else. I was the one who should have died. When she gave her life for me..." Skye's voice broke, and Bo put his arm around her.

Henrik had to escape this depressing conversation. He went

into the kitchen, opened the refrigerator and took out a soda. The sound of the can popping open echoed loudly through the quiet house. He walked over to his room and stopped at the door.

"Guess I'll go to bed now," he said.

"Here's some American slang for you," Bo said, breaking the heavy silence. "When we go to bed, we say "I'm going to hit the sack.' Not sure where that came from, but it's one way of saying it."

"Hit the sack," Henrik repeated. The strange words made no sense at all.

"Goodnight, Henrik," Skye said. "Shall I wake you in the morning?"

"I've got my alarm clock."

"Okay, sleep well."

"And don't listen to any screaming women," Bo added.

Screaming women? Oh yes, the stupid peacocks.

Late on the following evening, Henrik was lying in bed recalling his first day at Rolling Prairie High School. Bo and Skye had gone someplace—-he couldn't remember where—-and he'd stayed home. Before he went to his room he'd written a note and left it on the table. The note said, "I've hit a sack. Goodnight." He hoped they wouldn't bother him when they returned home.

There were a few things about school that looked promising: Winston and some of the other guys, one or two of the girls, the food at lunch and band. But there were other things that Henrik found depressing, like some of the teachers, American History, American Government and too many rules. There were rules about being late for class or leaving class; rules against what they called bad language; rules about "displays of affection" in the hallways; rules against smoking on the school grounds. There were even rules dictating what you could and couldn't wear, for heaven's sake!

It wasn't like that back home. He couldn't understand why the school had to regulate everything the students did. He'd asked Winston about it, and the answer he'd gotten was, "Who knows?" He'd asked if people got away with breaking the rules, and the answer was "Sometimes." He'd asked what happened if a guy got caught, and the answer was "It depends on what you did, and what the principal decides to do with you." And this was the United States? "The land of the free and the home of the brave"? Unbelievable!

A couple of the girls looked interesting. It was easy to tell the "wholesome Mattie's" from the girls who liked to party and knew how to have a good time. Winston would be helpful in that area too.

School lunches were new to him, but at least the food was good. Having a school band was also different. Swedish schools concentrated on academics. Sports and music activities were organized within the community. He liked the idea of filling an hour of his school day with band.

According to the guys, when the days turned cool, football practices would be after school instead of before. It looked like he'd be spending the entire day at school. Well, there wasn't much else to do. He lived too far from real civilization to bike anywhere more interesting than the boring countryside. There was no place to dance, or party or hang out in Wellsford. There wasn't a train he could take to Vicksburg. There was nothing to do at home except watch TV and play stick with the obsessive, compulsive Zeb.

He'd had his physical after school. What a joke. The doctor checked his eyes, ears, mouth and nose, tapped his knee, listened to his heart and lungs, and asked if he had any health problems or injuries that would prevent him from playing football. He'd thought about answering "There's something wrong in my head if I'm going out for football," but he'd just shrugged and said he could play any sport he wanted. The doctor sent him on his way with a pink permission slip. Tomorrow he'd be on the football field.

The exchange organization had cautioned students against making negative comparisons of America to their own country, and to not refer to anything as bad, or strange or stupid. Instead, they should use the word "different." Well, so far, everything was very different.

What the. . . ?? Why was the alarm going off in the middle of the night? Henrik reached over and turned it off. The illuminated numbers on the clock read 4:45. Henrik groaned. Football practice.

Bo was standing next to the dining room table, grinning at the note in his hand, when Henrik emerged from his room. He looked up at Henrik. "Good morning!" he said. "How'd you sleep?"

"Fine." Bo was still grinning—on the verge of laughing, Henrik guessed.

"What's so funny?"

"You hitting a sack last night." Bo let out a hearty chuckle.

"What's funny about that?"

"Well, we say 'hit the sack,' not 'a sack'."

"I guess it makes a big difference—a or the," Henrik snipped.

"I guess it does," Bo chuckled.

Henrik took the orange juice out of the refrigerator, and slammed the door. Jerk. Sometimes Bo's sense of humor just hit him wrong. He didn't like people laughing at him.

"I'll go get the bike, " Bo said. "I'll take you whenever you're ready."

Henrik got his school things together and stepped out of the house into the humid early Kansas morning. Bo was sitting on the low-slung seat of the Harley, his long legs stretched in front of the cycle, looking for all the world like the stereotypes of "Harley man on Harley bikes." Bo handed Henrik a helmet.

"I don't want that."

"Sorry—you have to wear it."

"Why?"

"Because I'm responsible for you and because the organization says so."

"You're not wearing one."

"I'm old enough to do what I want and I'm not an exchange student," Bo chuckled.

"This is so stupid," Henrik said, dropping the helmet onto his head. He studied Bo on the bike and the small high seat behind him.

"I suppose I have to sit on that dinky high seat behind you."

"That's right. Let's go."

Henrik stretched his long right leg over the seat and sat down. His natural height and his elevated position made him tower over Bo's black head in front of him.

"Ready?"

"Yeah."

Bo put the bike in gear, opened the throttle, and Henrik felt himself being nearly sucked off the back as the Harley surged forward. He grabbed instinctively for Bo's shoulders, and he could feel them shaking. Bo was laughing. They roared down the lane and onto the road. Henrik had to admit, this was a cool ride. He'd have to borrow the bike sometime and take it for a spin himself.

Fifteen minutes later, they pulled into the parking lot of Rolling Prairie High School, and Henrik got off.

"Thanks," he said.

"No problem. Good luck."

Henrik walked toward the large brick building without looking back. The Harley rumbled back down the lane, and he heard every shift Bo made through the gears as he thundered down the road.

"What'd'ya think, Swede-man?" Winston stopped by the locker room bench where Henrik sat, tying his shoes. Henrik looked up and groaned. "I'm dead."

"You get used to it," Winston assured.

"No you don't," responded the guy further down the bench. "You never get used to dying out there. You just pray you'll win some games to make it worthwhile. Nothing worse than dying in practice every day and losing a game every Friday."

"Aw, Mitch, don't make it sound so bad. We don't want Swede quittin' before the season starts. We need a kicker."

"I'm not quittin'."

"Good."

"You play a lot of soccer in Sweden?" Mitch, the team quarterback, asked.

"Uh huh. And we ski, and sail, and play beach volleyball. Not much chance of doing any of that stuff around here."

"Nope," Mitch agreed. "At least not right here. You can go to Colorado to ski, and there's a lake near Vicksburg where people sail. And," he chuckled, "Wellsford has a sand volleyball court." Henrik had seen that volleyball court. A square sandpit with a single net stuck in the middle of the small city park.

"I'm used to playing volleyball on the beaches of Spain," he bragged. "And I've seen the court in Wellsford."

"Probably about as different as the girls in Spain from the girls in Wellsford, if you know what I mean," Winston said.

"Do I!" agreed Henrik, bringing a hoot of laughter from Mitch and Winston.

"You bring pictures? From Spain?" Winston wondered.

"Naw. But I should have. Something to remind me what

pretty girls look like. It's going to be a long year."

The guys laughed again. "There's a few here that aren't too bad," Winston remarked.

"Like . . ?"

"Like Mattie—you saw her in church Sunday, remember? Tall, dark hair, nice legs?"

"I remember—she took us to our seats."

"Only one problem with Mattie," Mitch said. "She won't let you get close. Probably never even been kissed."

"You've gotta be kidding."

"Nope. She's about as innocent as they come, Swede."

A slow smile spread across Henrik's face.

"You know what I think, Winston?" Mitch said. "I think Little Miss Morals Mattie is about to meet THE SWEDE."

"I always did like a challenge," Henrik agreed.

SEVEN

WITH his classic Nordic features and lean, muscular body, Henrik never had a problem finding a girl. He was so confident of his ability to attract any girl he wanted, he decided to make a bet with Winston and Mitch. He'd bet that by the end of the week, he would have Mattie going out with him. If he won, they'd have to get him some cigarettes. The thought of losing never occurred to him.

Before he could make the bet, luck in the form of Mattie herself smiled on him in American History class.

"Hi, Henrik," she said, sitting down at the desk next to his. "How's it going?"

"For my second day in an American high school, it's going great," he grinned. "I think I can handle most of the classes, but this one," he shook his head, "this one will probably be hard for you American kids, not to mention a foreigner.

"Hey, if you need help, just let me know," Mattie offered. "I'd be glad to help educate a foreigner."

The gods must be smiling on him. He'd have this girl in the palm of his hand before you could say "Rolling Prairie High School, home of the Cougars." And he'd get his cigarettes too.

"How's football?" Mattie asked. "I hear you're quite the kicker."

"Just get me in field goal range, that's all the team has to do."

Henrik flashed his best girl-winning grin and leaned closer to Mattie. "You'll be at the game, won't you? I'll kick the first one for you."

"Oh, I'll be there. Everybody goes to the games."

"Good. Then watch, and if I kick one, you'll owe me, right?"

"Oh, I don't know about that," Mattie said, shifting her eyes from Henrik to the front of the classroom.

Henrik followed her gaze and realized the teacher and most of the class were watching him and Mattie. He slumped down in his chair and returned their stares.

"Just making friends," he announced to his snickering classmates. "Isn't that what a good exchange student is supposed to do?"

He glanced at Mattie but her eyes were riveted on her American History book. Yep, he'd have her on a date by the end of the week. And with luck, he'd not only have a pack of cigarettes, he'd also have his hands on a cold beer by Saturday night. He'd just decided to add that to the bet.

Between football practice, seven hours of daily classes, homework, and spending a little time on the couch in front of the TV, Henrik's first week of school passed quickly. The heat was still terrible, but he was getting used to it. His classes were easy, except for history and government. Mattie continued to be friendly, Winston and Mitch had taken him up on his bet, and he was getting along okay with Bo and Skye. If a few more things worked out, it might not be such a bad year after all.

One of those things was finding a girl, and he'd already decided Mattie would be his first at Rolling Prairie High. She hadn't agreed she would "owe him one" when he kicked his first field goal, but he wasn't worried. He knew she'd want to go out with him when she saw all the kids congratulating their new kicker after the game.

Henrik smiled to himself as he put on his football uniform Friday evening. The pads and tight pants made him feel so— American. Excitement surged through him when the team ran out from the locker room onto the field, and the crowd of spectators began cheering for the Cougars. This was great! He'd show these Americans he was more than just another player; just get him within field goal range and he'd show them some kicking like they'd never seen before!

He looked for Mattie during the team warm-ups, then tried to capture her attention when he saw her walking toward the bleachers. She was with a group of kids, talking and laughing, and never even glanced in his direction. He couldn't believe it! Well, that would change. Just get him within field goal range!

The teams gathered along the sideline for the playing of the national anthem. That was something else which was different from Sweden, Henrik thought, as the crowd cheered at the end of the song. The teams went into their huddles for a last-minute psyche, then ran out onto the field. Henrik remained on the sideline. He didn't understand why the coach wouldn't let him kick off. That would also change by the next game, he figured.

Neither team scored during the first quarter. Winston made a couple of great tackles, and Mitch was good quarterback, but the Cougars weren't moving the ball deep enough into the other team's territory.

Early in the second quarter, Mitch passed to a receiver who caught the ball on their opponent's 30-yard line. That put them within scoring range, at least. Henrik began warming up his leg.

Three downs later, the Cougars had moved the ball two feet. Henrik positioned himself near the coach, knowing it was time to try for a long field goal. He adjusted his helmet and waited for the nod. It didn't come. The coach sent the other kicker in to punt the ball.

Mitch ran to the sideline and stood next to Henrik as the defense took over.

"I can't believe it," Henrik muttered to Mitch.

Mitch looked up at him. "What?"

"Why didn't the coach let me kick? I could've made the field goal."

"It would have been a pretty long attempt. Besides, it's early in the game," Mitch said, keeping his eyes on the field.

"Yeah, right," Henrik growled in disgust.

The second quarter ended with Henrik still on the sideline. Neither team had scored, but he was sure the Cougars would have a 3-0 lead if the coach had let him kick a field goal.

At half time, the talk in the locker room was all about blocking and getting receivers open and rushing plays. The coach mentioned almost every player in the room except him. Still feeling disgusted, Henrik followed the team back out to the field. He didn't even look to see if Mattie was watching.

The game was still scoreless at the end of the third quarter. The two big zeros on the scoreboard taunted the players on both teams. Henrik remained on the sideline, his irritation growing with each missed opportunity for a possible field goal.

The opposing team broke the deadlock early in the fourth quarter, scoring a touchdown on a long unexpected pass. They kicked the extra point, making the score 7-0. The Cougars had to put some points on the board.

The opportunity came with three minutes left in the game. Mitch called a quarterback keeper, Winston and several other guys threw crucial blocks, and the wiry little quarterback broke away from the field. The Cougar fans cheered him into the end zone, and the score was 7 -6. Elated, Henrik quickly stretched his leg. Surely he'd be going in to kick the extra point. But instead of going for one, the coach opted for a two-point running play. Henrik couldn't believe the call. Sure, if it worked they'd take a one-point lead. But if it failed, the game would probably be over.

They set up as if they were kicking, then at the last minute Mitch kept the ball and ran with it. A loud groan rose from the Cougar bench and the crowded bleachers when Mitch was tackled just short of the goal line.

Frustrated, Henrik kicked the wooden bench behind the row of players. Now with just over two minutes left in the game, the other team had possession of the ball. It would take some kind of miracle to pull this one out.

Three plays later, the Cougars recovered a fumble on their 40-yard line. The crowd exploded. They still had a chance to win the game. The Cougar coach called time out.

"Let's run the slide option on the first down," he said. "Then the chute on second down. Call time after that, Mitch, and we'll decide what to do next."

Henrik's stomach flipped. If they got within field goal range, this could be it. He'd wanted a chance to kick, but not under this kind of pressure.

"TEAR 'EM UP, COUGARS!" the team yelled in unison as they left the huddle.

Henrik went through his stretching exercises, his eyes glued to the action on the field. Mitch took the hike, faked right, slid left, and then threw the ball to one of the running backs that put his head down and churned out nine yards before he was brought down. Second down and one, with a minute and a half showing on the clock. On the next play the blockers were supposed to line up on the right side of the field, forming a "chute" for a running back to slip through. It worked for five yards. They had the first down. The spectators went crazy and so did the butterflies in Henrik's stomach.

"Time!" Mitch hollered to the official.

"Men, we need to get within field goal range," the coach rasped to the team clustered around him. "Mitch, pass option two. I want you blockers working like you've never worked before. Let's go!"

He'd said it. Coach had said field goal range. The reality hit Henrik like a hard blow to the ribs. He tightened his helmet strap. Pass option two called for Mitch to choose between passing if he saw an open receiver, or keeping the ball himself. A tall Cougar named Corbin was open over the middle downfield. Henrik held his breath as Mitch threw the ball in a perfect spiral, and then exploded with a yell when Corbin hauled it in, moments before being tackled. Henrik looked at the clock. Forty-five seconds and counting.

"Time!" the coach yelled. "Mitch, come here!" Mitch and the rest of the team sprinted off the field toward their coach. The coach put his hand on Mitch's shoulder. "We can't try a 45-yard field goal. You're gonna have to pass."

"I can do it, Coach!" Henrik exclaimed.

"What's the longest you've kicked in practice?"

"About 35," Henrik lied. Actually, it had been closer to 30 yards.

The coach hesitated, then looked straight at Henrik and said, "All right, Swede, we're counting on you. Go do it."

"TEAR 'EM UP COUGARS!" the team yelled and sprinted onto the field. The crowd roared in anticipation. Henrik's heart was pounding. His shoes felt funny—he wasn't used to football shoes. He wasn't used to kicking a football, for that matter. He'd only attended three practices. He had no business being out here with the whole team counting on him. He paced off the steps and waited. The crowd had suddenly grown quiet. Henrik's legs were shaking.

"Hike, Hike!" Mitch's voice rang out clearly in the tense silence. He took the ball from the center and held it upright on the ground. Henrik began his stride. Right foot...left foot...right foot. His left foot slid inside the shoe. He reached with his right foot and felt it connect with the ball, and at the same instant, he was lying flat on his back. He couldn't breathe, and he couldn't see. Whoever was on top of him was heavy and disgusting.

"Get off me!" he yelled. "Get your fat ass off me!"

The player who'd tackled him laughed. "Welcome to American football, Swede!" he said, getting up slowly.

The game was over. They'd lost. Henrik rose slowly to his feet. His ribs hurt. His shoulder hurt. His pride hurt. The crowd was silent as he started to trudge off the field.

"Henrik!" yelled Mitch, running toward him. "There was a flag! The defense was offside! You get to kick again!"

Great, he got to kick again. His shoulder was killing him, his ribs hurt so bad every breath was agony, some fat guy on the other team was waiting to flatten him and he had to do it all over again. The fans had seen the signal from the officials, and now the noise from the bleachers was deafening.

The team lined up. The penalty brought the Cougars five yards closer to the goal posts. Henrik stepped it off. Pain had replaced the butterflies in his stomach.

"Hike, hike!" Mitch called. Mitch had the ball. He set it on the ground. Henrik took five steps. Right, left, right, left, KICK!

It felt good. Solid, straight and true. Suddenly, the pigskin started to veer. The wind! The fierce Kansas wind was pushing it to the right! Henrik watched in dismay as the football hit the inside of the right goal post and fell to the ground.

Was the kick good? Nobody knew. The teams and crowd hung in suspense, all eyes focused on the officials conferring in the end zone.

Finally, one of the men in the black and white shirts emerged from the group and faced the field. He raised his arms straight up.

Good! The field goal was good!

The crowd went crazy and the euphoric Cougars surrounded Henrik and carried him off the field. His whole body hurt, but oh, did it feel good!

Mattie was among the group of students waiting outside the locker room when the team emerged after their showers. Henrik walked over to her.

"Hey, Mattie, told you'd I'd kick one for you," Henrik grinned. "Even won the game just for you." To be honest, he hadn't thought about her at all when he made the kick.

Mattie smiled. "It was a great kick, Henrik. But you didn't do it for me, you did it for the team."

"The team and you," he insisted. "So, what are you doing now? Wanna go out with me and Winston?"

"Oh, no thanks, I've got plans with the girls."

"The girls? You'd rather go out with the girls than with me?"

"I guess so, Henrik. Thanks anyway."

He couldn't believe it. Girls just didn't turn him down like that. "What's up? I thought we had a deal. I kick a field goal for you—you go out with me."

"No, Henrik, you had a deal. I never agreed to it."

Winston sidled up to them, but before he could say anything, Henrik turned from Mattie and said, "Let's go, Winston. This chick has other plans."

"Told ya," Winston said, as they walked away.

"Shut up," Henrik hissed.

EIGHT

HENRIK could barely move when he tried to get out of bed the next day. His ribs and shoulder hurt like hell. Too bad it was Saturday. He'd have to wait until Monday to hear the kids say how cool it was that he'd won the game for the Cougars. At least he got to sleep in. After a week of pre-dawn practices, he deserved a few extra hours of sack time. The clock on the table next to his bed said 1:00. He really had slept in!

Skye was loading the dishwasher when he came out of his bedroom. She looked up and smiled. "Good afternoon!"

"Yeah," he said, rubbing his shoulder. "Man, I'm hurtin' today."

"Your first time on the field, and you get nailed. I never did like football."

"Don't know if I do either," he said, shuffling toward the fridge. He pulled out the pitcher of orange juice and poured himself a glass.

"Can I get you some breakfast, or lunch?" Skye asked.

"Sure."

"Cereal and fruit if it's breakfast, a turkey sandwich if it's lunch. Your choice."

His own mom in Sweden would make him a big meal, he thought. Americans seemed to exist on small, fast-food meals. They never seemed to have time to prepare a nice meal and sit down to eat it. Henrik didn't like cereal and fruit and he wanted more than a sandwich.

"Do you have pasta?" he asked.

Skye opened a cupboard and took out a package of spaghetti. "How about this?"

"Yeah. Pasta would be good."

"I'll get it started, but I've got a magazine calling me in a few minutes for an interview, so you may have to finish it yourself."

"I'm not sure I know how."

"It's pretty easy. Just follow the directions on the back of the box. Sorry, Henrik, but we had lunch at noon and you weren't up yet. I don't have time to operate a full-service restaurant any time of day." Skye's green eyes gazed directly into his.

Henrik turned and walked back into his room, closing the door hard behind him.

After his meal of spaghetti, Henrik spent the afternoon in his room, listening to music through his headphones and pretending to do homework while he nursed his physical and emotional wounds. Skye knocked on his door around 5:00 and asked if he was okay.

"Yes," he answered, opening the door. "I'm fine."

Then she asked if he would like to go with them to Dawdi's for the evening. He and Grandma were planning to have a farm auction, and family members were getting together for supper. Afterward, they would look through the sale items for things they wanted to buy before the auction.

"Should be some good food there," Skye smiled, and he knew she understood what he'd been thinking earlier.

"Won't it be hot in the house?"

"Yes, but we'll spend most of the time in the basement, which is a lot better."

"Okay," he said. Not his idea of a great Saturday evening, but it was better than hanging around home.

Later, on their way to Dawdi's in the pickup, Bo asked Henrik if he knew what Winston and some of the other guys were doing that evening. No, he didn't.

"You're welcome to invite them over anytime to watch movies or hang out at our place," Bo said.

"I thought maybe they'd ask me to do something with them," Henrik answered. "I thought Americans were supposed to be so friendly."

Bo and Skye exchange glances in the front seat. "People around here usually are very friendly," Skye replied, "but you'll probably have to take the initiative. They have friends they're used to doing things with, so you may have to invite yourself the first few times."

He didn't get it. A guy pays a lot of money to be an exchange student, and then he has to make his own meals and beg people to be his friends. What kind of deal was that? He shifted his position on the narrow back seat of the pickup.

"Yeah, I guess so," he said.

"Which reminds me," Bo said. "Skye and I are going to a Harley rally in the middle of September. We'll need to find a place for you to stay that weekend, or I guess you could stay home alone or have one of the guys stay with you, if you want."

Now that sounded promising. He certainly didn't want to go stay with somebody—-he wasn't some little kid who needed looking after. But the idea of having the place to himself created some interesting possibilities. Maybe that would be the time to invite a few kids over for a party, he thought, smiling to himself. "I'd like to stay home. I could feed the animals," he said, thinking that should sweeten the deal a bit.

"That would be great," Bo rumbled. They'd reached Dawdi's farm, and Bo turned the pickup into the lane. Several horses hitched to black buggies were already in the yard. More of Skye's relatives he'd have to meet. What a fun way to spend a Saturday night, he thought.

There were two houses in the farmyard. Henrik followed Bo and Skye toward the one belonging to Skye's Aunt Emma and her husband, Caleb. Emma was the youngest daughter of Jonas and Sue Ann and, in Amish tradition, she and her family lived next to her parents so they could provide any assistance needed by the elderly couple during their declining years.

Strange, Henrik thought. He seemed to be the one on exhibit, rather than these people in their odd clothes. They were even talking a different language, he noticed as he, Bo and Skye approached the small group of Amish men sitting at a picnic table under the trees.

"We'll stay out here with the men, Henrik," Bo said. "It's a little cooler out here with the breeze, and the women will let us know when the food is ready."

Skye gave Bo one of her "You men!" looks as she walked across the lawn and through the front door of the house. Henrik sat down in a lawn chair and tried to be inconspicuous, while Bo made himself at home at the picnic table.

"Hello, Bo," one of the bearded men said, switching to English.

"Hello, Caleb. How's it going?"

"It's going. Could use some rain."

"We could use anything that would cool it off."

Henrik listened while the men discussed the weather and talked about farming. He was hungry. The spaghetti he'd eaten for lunch was gone. He hoped Skye was right about there being lots of good food tonight.

The yard seemed to be full of children. Barefoot, sun-brown, the boys in long pants with suspenders and cotton shirts, the girls in simple dresses and the ever-present little white caps on their heads. Four kids were jumping on a trampoline near the house, several others were carrying around kittens, and three more were perched in the tree near the picnic table. Henrik looked up at them—two boys and a girl—and they smiled shyly back at him.

Soon an Amish woman stepped out of the house and announced that the meal was ready. Henrik followed the men as they made their way into the house. The three kids scrambled down from the tree, giggling as they fell in step behind him. Henrik turned and looked at them.

"So, what are your names?" he asked. Silence. Three innocent faces looked up at him. "My name's Henrik, but some people call me Swede," he continued.

More giggles, then the girl, who was about eight and apparently the oldest, said, "I'm Gwen."

"Hi, Gwen. Pleased to meet you," Henrik stuck out his hand, and shook her small tan one. Still more giggles.

"This is Glendon," she continued, putting her arm around the boy with her same sun-bleached hair and brilliant blue eyes. "He's my brother."

"Hello, Glendon," Henrik shook his dirty, little-boy hand.

"This is Kevin," Gwen said.

"Hi Kevin, how are you?"

"Fine," was the quiet answer.

"Is he your brother, too?"

"No, he's our cousin."

They entered the house and made their way down the stairs to the basement. Henrik immediately felt the difference in temperature, thinking it must be ten degrees cooler than outside. The basement was a single large room, unfinished, with concrete walls and no furniture except tables and benches. When everyone had descended the stairs, one of the Amish men said, "Let's pray."

Henrik assumed "Let's pray" meant someone would pray aloud. Instead everyone bowed their heads in a long, long silent prayer. He wondered how people knew when it was over. Finally,

one of the Amish men—probably the one who started it—
shifted his weight, cleared his throat, and made some noise. Then
they knew the prayer was over.

People began moving around and talking, and Henrik heard
Skye raise her voice and address the group. "While we're all here
together, I'd like to introduce the new member of our family."
Henrik felt everyone's eyes settle on him. "That tall guy over
there—that's Henrik Svensson," Skye continued. "He's from
Sweden, and he's going to be with us for this school year."

"Hello," he said, giving a half wave. He felt silly. The things
a guy had to go through to get a good meal.

The children were lining up at a long table laden with food.
The older ones served themselves, while mothers helped the
younger ones fill their plates. He wished they'd hurry——he was
starved.

"Go ahead, Henrik," Skye called to him from across the
room. "You're the biggest of the children."

Several of the adults and children laughed as Henrik stepped
into the line behind the girl named Gwen. She looked back up
at him and smiled.

"I'm pretty hungry, Gwen, so you'd better leave some food
for me," Henrik kidded.

"I will," she answered sweetly.

Skye was right. This was a spread. There were pans of what
looked like homemade pizza, bowls of watermelon and bowls of
salads, including several delicious-looking pasta dishes. And
desserts—a chocolate cake, several kinds of pies and an ice cream
and cookie thing he surely had to try. Henrik's mouth watered as
he filled his plate. When it was full, he piled on a second layer.
Then he followed Gwen to another table and folded himself
onto the bench next to her.

Bo leaned over, looking at Henrik's plate. "Good heaven's,
Henrik, you make it look like we don't feed you at home," his

low voice rumbled. Henrik took a bite out of the homemade pizza. "What can I say?" he answered, and kept right on eating.

Dawdi, standing nearby waiting his turn in the food line, chuckled softly. "Henrik, you come over any time you aren't getting enough food over there with Bo and Skye. We're not so far away. You can even walk over."

Henrik looked up at the friendly old man with the long white beard. One minute he thought the old geezer was off his rocker, and the next he seemed so perceptive and genuine. But if good Amish cooking was attached to getting to know him better, it would be worth the effort.

"I just might do that," he said.

"Good. We're getting ready to have a sale. We could use a pair of strong arms to help move things around."

He should have known there'd be strings attached.

NINE

FOR THE FIRST TIME in months, Henrik was looking forward to something. He hadn't really wanted to come to the United States and after his arrival, the next ten months stretched endlessly ahead of him. Now he was eagerly anticipating a break from his everyday routine. He could hardly wait until the second Friday in September when Bo and Skye would leave for the Harley-Davidson rally.

The house was empty when Winston brought him home from the football game that night. The kind of empty that said, "This place is yours for two whole days and it's time to party!"

Henrik told a few of the guys he'd have the house to himself for the weekend, and invited them over after the game. He didn't say anything else, figuring the rest would take care of itself.

He and Winston had been home about an hour, hanging out on the porch, when Mitch's antique Ford pickup came roaring down the lane. The truck stopped in front of the house and Mitch jumped out.

"Hey Swede!" he yelled. "Where's the party?"

"Wherever you want it!" Henrik yelled back. "You got something to party with?"

"Do I!" Mitch opened the passenger door of his pickup and said, "Take a look." The cab was filled with cases of beer. Henrik whistled in amazement. "How'd you manage that?"

"Connections," Mitch laughed. "I've got ice here that's melting. You got a tub or something we can put the stuff in?"

The only tub Henrik could think of was the water tank for the sheep. They'd just have to do without water for one night. He told Mitch to back the truck up to the small red barn while he emptied the tank. It was quickly filled with ice and beer, and Henrik was sipping on his first can when a car loaded with kids turned into the lane. Soon the entire driveway was lined with cars and pickups. Kids he'd never even met were there. Well, Bo and Skye, you told me to make friends and have people over, he thought, laughing out loud.

Sometime after midnight the sound of a Harley-Davidson roaring to life penetrated the fog clouding his brain. Henrik staggered toward the house, and saw, not Bo and Skye as he'd feared, but a guy he didn't know straddling a bike that Bo had left parked in the garage.

"No, don't!" he croaked, but his words were lost in the roar of the engine. The guy and the cycle disappeared down the lane. Henrik leaned against a pickup parked across the drive, trying not to panic. "It's okay," he told himself. "Nothing will happen. He'll come back in a minute."

Sometime later, there was a loud crash at the end of the lane. In the silence that followed, Henrik heard a faint cry for help. His heart pounding, Henrik joined the crowd of kids running down the drive. His legs felt strange, like they were somehow disconnected from his body. Silent screams of fear and frustration filled his head. Somebody was hurt—bad! Was the guy dying? NO! It couldn't be! DAMN this party! Damn that guy for taking the cycle and Mitch for bringing the beer! Cursing and crying, Henrik stumbled along with the others. It seemed to take forever to reach the cycle and its rider lying in a tangled heap against one of the parked cars. Henrik stared at the scene in front of him, trying through his alcohol-induced stupor to comprehend what had happened. His stomach heaved. He leaned against the car and threw up.

The sun peeked over the horizon casting long, yellow rays across the yard. Henrik and Winston sat on the front porch, sipping coffee and staring into space. One of their classmates was in the hospital with a badly fractured leg and a dislocated shoulder. The Harley was damaged. Beer cans littered the yard. The sheep stood next to the fence, their persistent bawling shattering the quiet of early morning.

"What's with the stupid sheep?" Winston muttered.

"Who knows."

"When do Bo and Skye get back?"

"Tomorrow evening."

"Least you'll have time to clean up the yard."

"Yeah."

"You gonna be in trouble?"

"Sure. Aren't you?"

"Yeah. My parents thought I was just spending the night with you. The party won't go over very big."

"What'll they do to you?"

"Don't know. What will Bo and Skye do?"

"Don't know. The organization might even send me home."

"Really?"

"Sure. We aren't supposed to drink."

"Who said you were drinking?"

Henrik reached over and tapped Winston on the head with his coffee cup. "Knock knock. We had a party, remember?"

"Who said you were drinking?" Winston tapped Henrik on the head in return.

"You don't think I can get them to believe the party just sorta happened and I wasn't a part of it, do you?"

"I think it's worth a try if you don't want to go back to Sweden."

Henrik didn't answer. Would it really be so bad if they did send him back? He hadn't wanted to be here in the first place. He'd have to face his parents. They'd be angry at first, but they'd get over it and life would go on. At least he wouldn't have to spend nine more months in Kansas.

He stood up. "Guess we'll have to wait and see what happens. Come on, let's go do the chores. Those sheep are driving me crazy."

Henrik dreaded Bo and Skye's return, and yet it couldn't happen fast enough. Waiting to tell them about the party was as miserable as the actual event. When the Harley finally rumbled into the yard late Sunday afternoon, Henrik took a deep breath and met them at the door.

"Welcome home," he smiled. "Did you have a good time?"

"We had a great time," Skye replied with enthusiasm. She took off her helmet and shook out her long blonde hair. "How about you?"

"Well, it's kind of a long story," Henrik said.

"What happened?" asked Skye, her voice reflecting concern.

"Like I said, it's a long story. I think we'd better sit down and talk about it."

"Are you okay? Are the animals okay?" Bo wondered, looking around the yard.

"Yeah, I'm all right and so are the animals."

"Let's get something cold to drink and you can tell us what happened," Skye said.

They carried their drinks out to the deck. Bo and Skye sat down across from Henrik and listened without comment while he told his story. He told them that Mitch brought beer, that a lot of kids showed up, that one of them tried to ride Bo's cycle and crashed it and was now in the hospital. He didn't tell them he'd been drinking, and they didn't ask.

"Our philosophy was to trust you until you proved we couldn't. It's a bad deal when that trust gets broken so fast," Bo said when Henrik had finished. There was nothing Henrik could say to that.

"I'm having a real hard time with this," Skye said sharply. She stared at Henrik, her green eyes bright with anger. "I don't understand why you let this party happen. What I do understand, from very personal experience, is what alcohol can do to a person's life. It screws you up, Henrik. It screws with your mind, and it screws with your body. I lost a kidney because of alcohol." Skye paused. "And because of that, I lost a sister, too."

He felt sorry for Skye. He surely did. But, he thought, we're not talking a lifetime of drinking here—just a party.

"I know you're probably used to drinking at home," Skye continued, her voice softening. "But for ten months we're asking you to make good choices, and one of them is to stay away from alcohol. If that's asking too much..." her voice trailed off. "Anyway, I guess we'll have to call your area rep and see what he says should happen next."

"Whatever," Henrik said quietly. "I really am sorry about the cycle."

"Me too," Bo responded in his deep voice. "I'm sorry about the cycle, and I'm sorry that you couldn't say no right from the beginning. You could have made us look like the bad guys and said, 'Sorry Mitch, my host parents will kill me and I'll get sent back to Sweden if you bring a beer party here.' We would rather be the bad guys than come home to something like this."

"I know."

"Bo won't tell you this, Henrik, but he's put many long hours into restoring that cycle," Skye said. "Now it's wrecked."

"It can be fixed again, honey," Bo said. "Just be glad the kid's not hurt worse."

"I am glad for that," Skye replied, her anger returning. "Of course I'd rather have a hundred wrecked cycles than one seriously hurt kid. But Henrik, you need to understand the damage that was done here Friday night. Not just to the cycle, but to you, to our trust in you, and to your chance to have a good year here."

"I know."

There seemed to be nothing more to say. Henrik got up and went in the house to escape from the uncomfortable silence that followed. He turned on the TV and slouched onto the couch.

By Monday morning everyone at school had heard about the party. Many of the kids had been there, and they were all eager to tell their version of what happened. Some of the stories Henrik overheard were true, others were close to the truth, but a few were totally off the wall. He had no idea where some of the stuff was coming from, but one fact was inescapable: the party had been at his home while his host parents were gone, and he was largely responsible for what happened.

He'd known he'd be in trouble with Bo and Skye and with the student exchange organization. What he hadn't thought about was the football team. The coach had strict rules against smoking and drinking, and anyone who got caught would be suspended from the team. That wasn't fair, Henrik thought angrily. In Sweden, a guy's private life was his own business. Obviously, it was different in American high schools. He might as well go home. He just wasn't cut out for this strict, no-fun approach to being a teenager.

When the coach met with the team before practice and read the names of the players who were ineligible for the next game due to their attendance at the party, Henrik had already convinced himself that he didn't care. He'd probably be on his way back to Sweden, anyway. Neither did he care that most of the varsity players were on the list, which meant the next game would have to be played by the junior varsity team. Then the coach announced that all the ineligible players would be expected to attend daily practices to help the younger guys prepare for Friday's game. It seemed obvious the coach was exceptionally tough on the varsity that day, and Henrik hated every minute of the practice.

Winston took him home, and when they drove into the yard, Henrik noticed a strange car parked near the house. It took him a minute to realize that WRLDFRDS on the personalized tag stood for World Friends, the name of the student exchange organization.

"Well, here goes," he said to Winston as he opened the car door. "My area rep is here. Should be about as much fun as football practice."

"Good luck," Winston said.

Zeb followed Henrik to the house, the ever-present stick in his mouth. Henrik ignored him.

Bo, Skye, and his area rep, Kory, were sitting in the living room. They'd met before, at the Vicksburg airport and again at an orientation meeting. Kory seemed nice enough. He was in his mid-30's, short and dark-haired with a full beard and intense dark eyes. He stood and shook Henrik's hand.

"Hi, Henrik."

"Hello."

"We were just talking about Friday night, so why don't you tell me about it?"

Henrik sat down and repeated the story he'd told Bo and Skye. When he finished, Kory leaned forward, looked straight into Henrik's eyes and asked the question Bo and Skye had not. "Were you drinking, Henrik?"

What the heck. What did it matter? "Sure," he answered.

"And do you remember signing an agreement with World Friends that listed things you couldn't do while you are here, including drinking?"

"Sure, but..."

"But what?"

He couldn't say that he'd signed it because it was part of deal in coming here, that he didn't think he'd get caught, that he didn't think World Friends would be so strict about enforcing it. "Nothing," he answered, looking down at the floor.

He knew they were all watching him. Why didn't they just tell him to start packing?

"You're a good kid, Henrik," Kory was saying. "Bo and Skye like you, and they want you to have a great year here. You can have a great year. It's your choice. You've made a mistake, a very big one. Now you can choose to make good decisions from here on, or to mess up again and go home. It's up to you, Henrik."

They weren't going to send him home after all. Henrik wasn't sure if that was good news or bad.

TEN

THE REST OF THE WEEK inched slowly along, punctuated by the daily torment of football practice. The coach was out to prove a point to the players who'd been at the party. Henrik, more than the rest of the team, resented the punishment. If they'd sent him home as he'd hoped, he wouldn't have been subjected to this foreign idea of discipline.

A conversation he'd overheard between Bo and Skye early Tuesday morning only added to his frustration. They were on the deck, having their morning coffee, when he entered the kitchen. He was pouring himself some juice when he overheard them mention his name. Curious, he'd moved closer to the open door leading to the deck and listened to their conversation.

"...probably thought he'd get sent home," Skye was saying.

"I have a feeling he was almost hoping that would happen," Bo's bass voice agreed.

"But like Kory said, staying may be worse punishment than leaving," Skye added. "It forces him to deal with the consequences, and to decide whether to make his year with us a good one, or not."

"He's a nice kid. I'd like to see him stay." Bo stood up then, and Henrik slipped quietly back to his room.

The conversation bothered him for the rest of the week. He certainly didn't like being disciplined by people he barely knew.

But the thing that really bugged him was what Bo said about wanting him to stay. His negative attitude about living in Kansas had been obvious from the start, and he'd done very little to deserve Bo's kind words. Henrik was having a hard time understanding Americans.

As expected, with the junior varsity team playing, the Cougars lost the game Friday night. The varsity players watched from the sideline, glumly enduring their humiliation before the large crowd of family and friends filling the bleachers.

Unlike the week before, Henrik and the other players went straight home after the game. Not wanting to go to bed so early on a Friday night, he sat down at the computer and logged onto the Internet. He soon found a teen chat room, and spent the next several hours visiting with girls from other parts of the United States. It was 3:00 a.m. when Henrik finally signed off and went to bed.

He was sound asleep, dreaming of girls back home in Sweden, when someone knocked loudly on his door.

"Ja?" he answered in Swedish, barely awake.

"Henrik," Skye called. "Time to get up. I need to talk to you."

Henrik sat up, rubbing his eyes and shaking his head. The clock said 10:00 a.m. He got out of bed and shuffled to the door. Opening it a couple of inches, he looked past Skye and saw Dawdi sitting at the dining room table.

"Dawdi could use your help today, moving things to get ready for the sale," said Skye. "Do you think you could get ready and go with him?"

"I guess so," he muttered.

"Good. Thanks!"

"Grandma made fresh cinnamon rolls this morning," Dawdi called out. Henrik managed a smile. Okay, he was on his way.

A few minutes later, Henrik climbed onto the buggy seat beside Dawdi. The old man shook the reins and the horse trotted down the sandy lane. His first horse and buggy ride in Kansas. Kinda cool, he had to admit. September was quite nice, now that summer was almost over and the days weren't so hot. The mid-morning sun shone down on rusty red fields of ripening grain.

"What is that?" Henrik asked, pointing across the road.

"Milo," Dawdi answered. "It's a grain that's used for livestock feed. Don't you have it in Sweden?"

"Heck if I know. I never paid much attention."

"What crops do you have?"

"Where I live, we have forests, but we also grow some hay and other things—oats and potatoes. In the south they have wheat and other stuff like that."

"Your family, they are in the lumber business?"

"Yeah," Henrik said, impressed that Dawdi remembered. It had been more than a month since he'd told him about his family. "It's been our family business for years and years."

"Kinda like farming here."

"Has your family been farming here for generations?"

"Since the late 1800s. Some things are the same for us as they were then, but some things are changing."

Henrik couldn't imagine living the same way people did a century ago. But the clop-clop of the horse's hooves on the pavement were a reminder of what hadn't changed for the Amish. And then there were Dawdi's clothes, and...

"What's changed?" he wondered.

"More than you probably think," Dawdi turned to look at him with his clear blue eyes, a smile forming above his long, white beard. "It might seem to you like we're still living in the

1800s, but we've made some adjustments to technology."

"Like what?"

"Well, when Sue Ann and I got married, we had to decide between farming with horses or tractors. The Amish were split on that issue. We still are."

"What difference does it make?" Henrik hoped he wasn't being rude, but he wanted to know.

Dawdi was quiet for awhile, and Henrik was afraid that he'd offended him. "It's a good question," Dawdi finally replied. "Sometimes people who farm with tractors use them like cars. They drive them to town instead of their horse and buggy."

"And that's bad?"

"Bad? No. Wrong? In the eyes of God? No, I don't think so, although I wouldn't want to say what God is thinking."

"Then what's the big deal?"

Dawdi chuckled softly. "You aren't the first to ask that question, Henrik. What's the big deal? The most important things for us Amish are our families and our church life. Modern technology has a way of sneaking in and taking over families. We don't want that."

"How?"

"Like the telephone. We use it. It's a handy thing to have. But if you have a telephone in your house, it controls your life. When it rings, you have to answer. Children spend time on the telephone talking with friends rather than playing with their brothers and sisters. So we have phones outside—like the one in the hedgerow over there—so we can use them but they don't control us."

Henrik noticed a small white building in the row of trees along the road. So that was an Amish phone booth.

"It's the same with cars," Dawdi went on. "We hire people to drive us places. We don't think cars themselves are bad. But if you own a car, it's much easier to go farther away from your family and church community than if you use a horse and buggy."

"So it isn't really a religious reason, is it?"

Dawdi took awhile to answer. A bird sang from a fence post as they drove by, and Henrik realized he would never have heard it in a car.

"If you mean is there a place in the Bible that says 'Thou shalt not own a car,' then, no, it isn't a religious reason. But the Bible talks about honoring our parents and the importance of bringing up our children to be God-fearing people. We believe that having too many worldly things affects family life, so that does make it a religious reason.

"I'm not saying that a car is wrong for you, Henrik," Dawdi continued. "What is important is that you honor your parents and how you were brought up. I was raised Amish and for me, that means following the traditions that have been ours for many generations. Does that make sense?"

"Yeah," Henrik nodded.

The horse slowed and turned into Dawdi's lane. Henrik was almost sorry their short trip was over. He was actually enjoying the time with Dawdi, hearing why he believed what he did. It all seemed strange, but it did make sense in its own way.

"I've been doing all the talking," Dawdi said. "What about you? Do you and your parents have certain beliefs? Which church do you go to in Sweden?"

Henrik's regret quickly changed to relief. He didn't want to talk about his church and what he believed. He wouldn't know what to say. He wasn't sure he had any "beliefs" and he didn't want to tell this kind, religious man that his church attendance in Sweden was pretty much limited to Christmas and Easter.

"Maybe we'll talk about that later," Henrik said. "I think I smell those cinnamon rolls, and you know I can't work until I have at least two of them."

"Yah, we'll have more time to talk, and I'm ready for a roll myself," Dawdi agreed as the horse stopped at the hitching post near the house.

Henrik consumed two large cinnamon rolls dripping with frosting and a tall glass of milk, then followed Dawdi outside. Behind the barn was a row of horse-drawn farm implements, and beyond that were stacks of tin, rolls of wire, piles of posts, and other farm items.

"We need to move these things out and sort them into smaller groups to sell," Dawdi explained. "I'm just too old to do it by myself, but we can get a lot done together."

Dawdi started out trying to help, but when he began breathing hard as they carried a large post together, Henrik suggested that he handle it alone. The last thing he wanted was Dawdi dying on him out there from a heart attack. So, for the next hour and a half, Henrik moved tin, rolls of wire, and hedge posts into neat piles. Near noon, as he picked up one of the posts, a sharp stab in his hand made him drop the post to the ground. A small pool of blood was collecting in the palm of his hand, and it hurt like crazy. *Stupid post must have had a nail in it*, he realized. He walked over to where Dawdi was sitting on a tree stump, watching.

"Got a little injury here," Henrik said, showing Dawdi the bloody hand.

"You sure do," Dawdi said, pulling a faded red bandanna out of his pants pocket. "Here, wrap this around it and we'll go inside. Grandma will give you something to clean it and a bandaid. I hope you've had your tetanus shots."

"Yeah, we had to make sure we had them before we could come as exchange students," Henrik winced. How could a small hole hurt so bad?

"I don't want to get your handkerchief all bloody," he said.

"No problem. That's what they're for—to be used. You ask Skye sometime to tell you about her red handkerchief."

"Okay, I will," Henrik concentrated on wrapping the bandanna around his hand.

Henrik smelled Grandma's fried chicken as they entered the house, and realized he was hungry again. Several minutes later, after bravely enduring whatever it was Grandma dabbed onto his hand, he let her put a bandaid on top and wrap it with gauze tape. Then he was ready to eat.

The smells of Grandma's cooking tantalized him through the long silent prayer, and when Dawdi finally cleared his throat and moved slightly in his chair, Henrik wasted no time forking food onto his plate.

"Help yourself, young man," Dawdi laughed.

"He's a growing boy and needs a lot of food," Grandma defended. "You just eat all you want, Henrik."

"I heard you had quite the doings at your house last Friday night," Dawdi said, scooping mashed potatoes onto his plate.

Henrik's heart skipped a beat, and he paused between forkfuls of homegrown corn. "Yeah, you might say that."

"Young people always seem to want to have parties and drink beer," Dawdi continued.

Great, here comes the sermon, Henrik thought.

"Remember that, Grandma?" Dawdi looked at his wife and Henrik could have sworn he winked.

"That was a long time ago, Dawdi," she answered.

"Maybe so, but like I was telling Henrik on the way over, some things change and some don't. Teenagers having parties doesn't seem to change."

Dawdi looked across the table at Henrik and continued, "Grandma here—she's older than me by two years. She'd been at parties for two years before I turned 16. So I had to learn from her. Isn't that right, Grandma?"

Henrik looked at the prim little Amish woman with her starched white head covering and dark blue dress sitting beside him. Dawdi surely must be joking, he thought. Sue Ann's dark eyes rested fondly on the face of the man across the table from her. A kernel of corn had settled into his white beard near his chin.

"Isn't that right, Sue Ann honey?" Dawdi repeated, his dancing eyes meeting hers. "Tell Henrik about the parties."

ELEVEN

"DAWDI CAN TELL YOU about the parties, Henrik," Grandma turned to look at the tall, young Swede seated at the table next to her. "Not only is he a better storyteller than I am, he has more stories to tell!"

Dawdi chuckled and reached for the plate of homemade bread. "Yah, I could tell you stories, Henrik. Some are funny, and some are sad. That's the way it is with teenagers. Sometimes they find ways to have fun that are harmless, but other times someone gets hurt...or even killed. I'm sure it's that way in Sweden, too."

Henrik nodded. "So what did you do for fun? Race your buggies?" he asked jokingly.

"Sure, we did that all the time. I had a fast horse—his name was Lightning. We could beat almost any of the other guys and their horses. But Lightning couldn't pop a wheelie like one horse could."

"Pop a wheelie?"

"You know, get the front wheels up in the air. One guy could get his horse real excited while he was standing still, then he'd slap the reins and yell, and that horse would jump forward fast enough to lift the buggy wheels right off the ground."

"Really!" Henrik had trouble visualizing how a horse could do that.

"Tell him what happened with Lightning and the buggy that

4th of July when we were going steady," Grandma urged.

"Now that was a good one," Dawdi leaned back in his chair. "I lived here in a mobile home before we got married and built this house. We'd gone to town that night to watch the fireworks. When it was time to go home, we went back to where I'd tied Lightning, but he and the buggy were both gone. Scared us half to death, wondering how he'd gotten loose, and if he was running around town, pulling the buggy. Then some of the guys showed up and offered to take us home."

"They'd been drinking, and I didn't want to ride with them," Grandma added.

"But what else could we do? We got in the back of the truck and hoped for the best. When they drove into the yard, we saw our buggy," Dawdi paused for emphasis. "We saw our buggy sitting on top of the house."

"On top of the house? How'd it get there?"

"You'd be amazed what a bunch of kids can do," Dawdi laughed. "And that wasn't all. Guess where Lightning was."

"I don't know."

"That horse was inside the mobile home, just standing there in the living room."

Laughter bubbled from the elderly, conservative Amish couple and the worldly, resentful Swedish teenager sitting together at the table.

Before leaving for church the next morning, Henrik walked out to the pasture to check on the sheep. The new fall lambs had begun arriving the week before, and the ewes needed to be checked several times a day. Henrik had volunteered his help, knowing it would make a favorable impression on Bo and Skye. It was also the perfect opportunity to sneak a cigarette from the pack Winston had given him. Henrik knew that if he got caught violating the organization's rules a second time, he would probably be sent home. But the way he figured it, sheep can't talk, so he'd never have a problem.

The Mennonite youth group was having a party at the church that evening. Henrik didn't think it would be much fun, but Bo and Skye urged him to go, and Mattie Smucker had offered to pick him up and bring him home afterward. Not exactly a real date, Henrik reasoned, but better than spending another boring night at home.

There were about twenty kids gathered in the youth room at the church when Henrik and Mattie arrived. Several were operating video cameras, taping the antics and conversations of the others.

"What are we doing tonight?" Henrik asked Mattie.

"Something with video cameras, but I'm not sure what," she answered, grinning.

The youth leaders asked the kids to be quiet while they explained the evening's activity. They would be divided into three groups. Each group would be given a camera and a list of things to tape. They would have an hour and a half to complete the list and return to the church to show the others what they'd recorded. Not as much fun as a beer party, Henrik thought, but better than listening to a speaker talk about God.

With luck and a bit of maneuvering, he managed to be in Mattie's group. He slid into the front seat of her car and looked at the list she handed him. When the rest of the group had climbed into the back seat, he read the list aloud.

1. Flower power
2. You clean those dentures
3. The name of the game
4. Guy in old lady clothes
5. Give it your best shot

6. Wedding pictures
7. Up a creek without a paddle
8. Owner/dog look-alikes
9. Fried egg
10. Board chair

"This should be fun!" Mattie laughed when he finished, and the other three youth in the back seat echoed her response.

"How are we supposed to do this?" Henrik wondered.

"It'll probably be best to pick on family and church people who know us. We choose somebody we think can help us get what we need, tape it, and go on."

"We go someplace and ask the person to clean their dentures while we tape it?" Henrik couldn't decide if this was stupid or just plain silly.

"Is that what it says?"

"It says 'You clean those dentures.'"

"Then I think it means you clean somebody else's dentures."

"No way."

Mattie laughed again. Maybe this evening would turn out to be fun after all, Henrik thought.

Mattie parked in front of a well-kept yard in Wellsford, and they all walked up to the house. Mattie rang the bell and a tall, heavy-set woman came to the door. She looked through the screen at Mattie.

"Hello, Tina. Our youth group is on a video scavenger hunt, and we were wondering if we could borrow one of your dresses for a few minutes."

"You want one of my dresses?" the woman repeated, eyeing the group of kids standing behind Mattie. "What are you going to do with it?"

"That tall, blond guy is going to put it on," Mattie said, pointing to Henrik standing at the back of the group. "He promises not to damage it at all. As soon as he has it on, we'll tape him, and then you can have the dress back."

"Why me?" Henrik asked.

"You have to do something," Mattie answered, "and you won't brush dentures, so you might as well do this."

The woman surveyed the group again, then opened the door and invited them inside. Moments later Henrik was in the bathroom, stripped to his boxer shorts, slipping on a pink flowered polyester dress. He heard wolf whistles on the other side of the door, and the chant, "Swede! Swede! Swede!" He sprayed himself liberally with some cologne he found next to the sink, and wondered what his friends back home would think if they could see him now. Henrik opened the door, flashed his sweetest smile, fluttered his eyelashes and sashayed into the room.

When Mattie took him home later that evening, they laughingly recalled some of the highlights from the scavenger hunt.

"Poor Winston had to let his mom poke him in the arm for 'Give it your best shot,'" Henrik laughed. "At least his mom's a nurse and knew what she was doing."

"I liked the owner/dog look-alikes," said Mattie, "Especially the one where Cassie's group dressed Rannie's dog in a referee's shirt, put a whistle around his neck, and held a picture of Rannie in front of the dog's face."

"Yeah, that one was funny, too."

"But my favorite was when you came out of Tina's bathroom looking and smelling like a big, flirty old woman! I thought I'd die laughing."

"I'd forgotten about the perfume," Henrik chuckled. "I bet Bo and Skye will wonder what I've been doing tonight!"

"I'll be glad to come in and explain it to them," Mattie offered.

"You won't need to do that," Henrik said, then realized he'd just passed up the chance to spend more time with Mattie. "But if you want to come in and help me tell them about the evening, that'd be cool," he added.

"Sure, I'd like that," Mattie replied.

Bo and Skye seemed pleased to see Mattie enter the house with Henrik. Bo invited them into the family room and Skye offered them soft drinks. Henrik had never seen Bo or Skye laugh as hard as they did when Mattie described his debut as a "big, tall, cologne-soaked, flirty old woman."

"I would've given anything to see you," Bo chuckled.

"Something else you should have seen," Mattie continued, "was the look on Henrik's face when we did a Chinese fire drill."

"We're driving along, and all of a sudden she just stops the car, screams 'Mennonite car dance!' and everybody gets out and runs around the car!" Henrik explained. "I sat there wondering what in the world they were doing. Then they all get back in the car, laughing their heads off, and Mattie drives on down the road. A few miles later, they do it again."

"Only this time we made him come along," Mattie giggled.

"Yeah, so I ran around the car with them. But what was the point?"

Mattie, Bo and Skye laughed heartily, and Henrik joined in. They continued talking about the scavenger hunt and suddenly Henrik realized how much he was enjoying himself. For the first time, he was truly happy to be in Kansas.

All too soon, Mattie looked at her watch and said she had to get home.

"Thanks for giving me a ride tonight," Henrik said, walking her to the car.

"No problem," she answered, opening the door and sliding behind the wheel. Henrik rested his arm on top of the door, holding it open. He smiled down at Mattie as she looked up at him to say good-bye. Here was his chance.

"Hope you don't mind kissing a guy that smells like an old woman," he said, leaning toward her.

"Henrik, no," Mattie said softly, gently touching his face with her hands.

Surprised, he pulled back and asked, "Why won't you give me a little kiss?"

"I like you Henrik," Mattie answered. "But I hardly know you. I don't kiss guys I hardly know."

Give me a break, Henrik thought. "Fine," he said, stepping back and closing the door. Why did he even bother with this girl?

"See you in school tomorrow," Mattie said as she started the car.

"Yeah, sure," he muttered, watching her tail lights disappear down the lane.

He stared up at the stars glittering in the black sky overhead and wished for a good old Swedish girl who didn't have hang-ups about kissing a guy she "hardly knew." A girl and a smoke, that's what he needed. Time to go check the sheep.

Bo was waiting on the deck when Henrik returned to the house thirty minutes later.

"Any new lambs?" the low voice asked.

"Nope."

"Henrik."

"Yeah?"

"You smell like smoke. Sheep don't smoke."

Henrik's heart turned a somersault, then sank to the bottom of his stomach.

"We'll keep it between us, if you wash all of your clothes that smell like smoke, and if you quit now. If I smell it again . . ." Bo left the rest of the sentence unspoken, but Henrik knew how to finish it: ". . . the organization will be booking your flight home."

TWELVE

HE DIDN'T WANT TO GO HOME. For the first time since he'd arrived in Kansas, Henrik hated the idea of being sent back to Sweden. He wasn't sure what had happened to change his mind, but part of it was his success as a kicker on the football team. Part of it was the friends he'd made with the guys at school. And Mattie figured in there somewhere, although he had no idea why he was wasting his time on a girl who wouldn't kiss him.

Then there was his growing relationship with Bo and Skye, and Dawdi and Grandma Bontrager. Bo and Skye were cool host parents. They were easier to live with than his own parents, which was also hard to explain. He could do a lot more at home, like drink and smoke and stay out all night with his friends. But his natural parents were so wrapped up in the family business that they didn't have time for him, except to yell when he was late for work. At least that's how it seemed to Henrik.

Bo and Skye had rules that seemed stupid and made him wonder if they thought he was still twelve years old. But despite the rules, it was the atmosphere in their home that made him realize he didn't want to leave. Bo's sense of humor had really grown on him, and Skye, with her rock star background, understood teenagers better than most mothers. They parented him with a kind, relaxed firmness that he was beginning to appreciate.

And who would have believed a few months ago that two

elderly Amish people would become so important to him. The old man intrigued Henrik, and he valued their growing friendship. Behind the long white beard and twinkling blue eyes was a lifetime of stories and experiences, and Henrik wanted to hear them.

His opportunity came in American History class on Monday morning.

"Today we're going to talk about a project that you'll be doing between now and the end of the semester," Mr. Estee, the teacher, announced. "American History isn't just about the people and events in the textbook. It's also about the people that settled this community and other communities where your ancestors lived."

Each student was to research one person in their family and either write a paper or present a talk to the class about that person, explained Mr. Estee. Great, Henrik thought. Nothing like doing research long-distance to Sweden.

"And Henrik, you may use someone from Bo or Skye's family if you want to," Mr. Estee said. "Personally, I think Jonas Bontrager would be a great resource." Henrik liked that idea. He glanced at Mattie, sitting in the desk to his right.

"That'd be cool, Henrik," she whispered. "I bet nobody else will get to interview an Amish preacher."

Henrik flashed her a thumbs up. "You wanna come along?" he whispered back.

Mattie smiled but shook her head no. Henrik pulled out a piece of notebook paper and wrote, "How about a date? What better chaperone could you want than an Amish preacher?"

He slid the paper across the aisle and onto Mattie's desk. Mattie suppressed a giggle as she read the note. Henrik grinned. He always did like a challenge when it came to girls. He wasn't giving up on this one yet.

Henrik hadn't had a cigarette all week, but he'd chewed a lot of gum and sucked on so much butterscotch candy his mouth was sore. He didn't have one after Friday night's game either. As much as he and the other guys wanted to celebrate their big win against their arch rival, they didn't have a party. They hadn't lost a game since the humiliation at the beginning of the year, and no one wanted to risk being kicked off of the team.

So they hung out in the city park after the game that evening, talking to the girls who stopped by and waiting for the town cop to send them all home when the city's midnight curfew rolled around.

"Dude, are you sweet on that Mattie chick or what?" Mitch asked Henrik as they stood leaning against Mitch's antique Ford pickup. "I know you are—I see you flirting with her in American History all the time."

"She's all right," Henrik admitted.

"Aw Swede, you're after her big time. Too bad you can't drive. She's gonna have to take you on a date. Won't that be special?"

"I'm sure it will—if it ever happens."

"Have you asked?"

"Sure."

"And?"

"And the first time she said no."

"And the second time?"

"Who says there was a second time?"

"You gotta keep trying, man."

The words were barely out of Mitch's mouth when Mattie's little white Dodge puttered up to where the guys were standing. Five giggling girls spilled out and, with Mattie in the lead, ran to the slide and climbed the steps. Halfway down Mattie stopped on the slide's hump, and the other four girls sandwiched up behind her. Their laughter grew louder, and one of them hollered, "Hey! Are there any men in the park?"

"Are there any men who could rescue some damsels in distress?" Mattie added dramatically.

The guys looked at each other.

"Cheap thrills," Mitch muttered.

"Poor substitute for a party," Winston agreed.

"Better than nothing," Henrik said.

"Easy for you to say. You'll take the cute one," Winston noted.

"You got that right." Henrik sauntered toward the slide and the other guys followed. He stood as close to Mattie as the playground equipment would allow, took her hand and said, "May I assist you, my dear damsel in distress?"

"Why, yes, you may, Prince Swede. That would be so kind of you."

"I will rescue you from this steel tower that holds you captive. Here, put your arms around my neck."

Before she could protest, Henrik put his arms around Mattie and lifted her from the slide. He felt her arms wrap around his neck, he smelled her perfume and heard her laugh quietly in his ear. He set her down slowly, and for a moment they stood looking into each other's eyes. In another place, with another girl, a kiss would have been natural. A long, luscious, drawn-out, body-trembling kiss, he thought wistfully. But not here and not with this girl.

"I've saved you from certain death on the playground tower," he said, searching her eyes. "Would you give me the pleasure of your company tomorrow when I go to talk to the old Amish man?"

"I would enjoy that very much, Prince Swede. What time will you pick me up in your carriage?"

Henrik stepped back, feigning frustration. "I'm afraid that my carriage is 'in the shop', as they say. Could you perhaps pick me up in your carriage?"

"I believe I could do that. Shall we say 1:00 p.m.?"

"Works for me."

The moment Henrik became aware of the stillness around them, it was broken with claps and cheers. How long had the other guys and girls been listening? He really didn't care.

"So, you want to use me for your research paper?" Dawdi pulled on his beard thoughtfully, and Henrik nodded. Dawdi, Grandma, Henrik and Mattie were sitting around the familiar kitchen table in the Amish home, drinking tall glasses of lemonade. On the table, near Henrik, was a small plate with one large cinnamon roll. It was just an hour past lunch, but that didn't affect his appetite for Grandma's rolls, he'd readily admitted when he walked in the door and saw them on the kitchen counter.

"That's right, Dawdi. Mr. Estee even said you would be a good person to talk to."

Dawdi chuckled. "I suppose I can talk if you want to listen. What do you want to talk about?"

"Oh, what it was like when you were growing up. Stuff like that. But I was kinda hoping to do the interview another time. Today, I was wondering if you'd take Mattie and me on a buggy ride." Henrik glanced at Mattie. He hadn't mentioned a ride to her, and he hoped she'd be happily surprised.

"Oh, that would be so much fun!" Mattie exclaimed. "I've never ridden in a buggy before!"

"It'll take me a little while to hitch up the horse," Dawdi said.

"Can we help?" Mattie asked.

"Oh, you can supervise," Dawdi said, standing up slowly and walking toward the utility room next to the kitchen. He took his straw hat from the hook near the door, and Henrik and Mattie followed him out the door.

They watched as Dawdi caught the horse and led him out of the corral. He left the horse standing, untied, while he went into the shed to get the harness.

"Isn't he going to walk away?" Henrik spoke to the retreating back of the old Amish man.

Dawdi stopped and turned. "Sailor? Naw. He's old. And he knows better."

He continued into the shed and emerged a few minutes later with the harness and a bridle. Dawdi moved with a slow certainty as he slid the bridle onto Sailor's head and arranged the harness over his back. He fastened the straps, then said, "Now if you want to, you can help pull the buggy out."

Henrik and Mattie followed Dawdi to the small building near the house. Inside was a shiny black buggy with a bright orange slow moving vehicle sign attached to the back. Henrik picked up the long pieces of wood attached to the front of the buggy and began to back it out. He was surprised how easily it moved, but then he realized it needed to, for a single horse to pull it with people inside.

"Now bring the buggy around behind Sailor and drop the shafts slowly across his back so he knows it's there," Dawdi instructed. "Mattie, you can get on one side."

So the long pieces of wood were called shafts, Henrik thought.

"Take it easy. Sailor probably won't spook if you poke him, but some horses would. Then you could have a runaway on your hands."

"Has that ever happened to you?" Mattie wondered.

"A runaway? Yeah. I guess it's the Amish version of a car accident. But we don't have nearly as many people getting killed as you do with cars. Percentage-wise, I mean."

"How about cars hitting horses and buggies? Don't you have serious accidents like that?"

"We do, but maybe not as much as you'd think. English people who live in Amish communities are usually pretty respectful of us and watch out." Dawdi was hooking up the buggy to the harness as he spoke. Then he took the long reins in his wrinkled hands and fed them through the front window of the buggy.

"Hop in," he said.

Mattie got in first, and the buggy tilted down toward her as she stepped on the metal footpad. Henrik followed her into the back seat, and his weight brought the buggy leaning toward him at a radical angle. It didn't seem very secure, that was sure. He was glad Sailor was a horse that wouldn't run away with them.

"Let's go, Sailor," Dawdi slapped the reins lightly across the horse's back.

"This is so cool," Mattie smiled up at Henrik. He grinned back and put his arm around her shoulders. In front of them, Henrik noticed that Dawdi was rubbing his chest and stomach.

"Are you okay, Dawdi?" he asked.

"Me? Yah. Must have had too many of Grandma's baked beans for dinner. Just some gas. It'll pass." Dawdi laughed at his own joke, but Henrik heard the strain in his laughter.

Henrik settled back into the seat with Mattie, but he was just a little bit worried.

THIRTEEN

PUFFY WHITE CLOUDS had been gathering all day, occasionally darkening the landscape below, then suddenly parting to let the mild October sun shine through. One moment there was promise of light and warmth and the next a dreary chill. Henrik had wanted a pretty day for the buggy ride with Mattie. He hadn't minded the gray skies of Sweden, but now that the intense heat of summer had passed, he'd learned to appreciate the endless days of Kansas sunshine.

The clouds had disappeared when they started the ride with Dawdi. The sun shone through the open window in the front of the buggy, played across Dawdi's face and teased Henrik and Mattie in the back seat. It was a friendly sun, not the searing hot summer rays that turned black Amish buggies into wooden ovens. No, this sun softly warmed the body against the upcoming cold of winter.

And winter's chill wasn't far away. Henrik and Mattie had barely begun to enjoy the warm rays when the clouds returned. Amazing what a difference it makes, Henrik thought. He wished for sunshine, but he didn't mind the excuse to hold Mattie just a little closer.

"Sure hope we have a nice day for the sale," Dawdi said, half turning his head toward the back seat.

"When is the sale?" asked Henrik, leaning forward. "You told me, but I've forgotten.

"Third Saturday in October. Three weeks from today."

"What is the weather like in late October? Does it snow?"

"Snow? No. It might be rainy and cold, but no snow. I can remember snow on Halloween once, but that was unusual."

They rode past fields fuzzy green with new winter wheat, and talked about the sale. Henrik asked if it was difficult to sell things that had been a part of their lives for so long.

"The hardest thing will be my team of work horses," Dawdi said. "We've spent many hours together, but I'm not using them anymore. They need to go to somebody who will use them."

"Will another Amish man buy them?" Mattie asked.

"Maybe. Or maybe somebody who wants to use a team for wagon rides, parades, and things like that. Red and Fred are a matched pair of Belgians, and they're completely safe. I 'spect there'll be quite a few people interested in them."

The sun continued its cat and mouse game with the persistent clouds. Toward the end of another mile, Dawdi asked, "How far do you want to go?"

Henrik could have ridden that way for a long time, his arm around Mattie, listening to the relaxing clop-clop-clop of Sailor's hooves striking the pavement.

"I have to get back before too long. I have another commitment," Mattie answered.

"What? You have another date after this one?" Henrik drew back in mock disgust.

"Yeah, with the youth group executive. We're having a planning meeting."

Dawdi turned the buggy around at the next intersection and they headed back to his farm. The sun finally gave up and retreated behind the thickening gray clouds racing across the sky. Henrik wondered if the rain would come before Dawdi got the horse unhitched and the buggy put away.

"Do you need to leave with Mattie?" Dawdi asked Henrik after they'd unhitched Sailor and pulled the buggy back into the shed. The rain held off, but the air felt damp and heavy.

"No, I guess not. Why?"

"Oh, I thought we'd sit down with some of Grandma's warm church cookies and talk about that research paper of yours."

Henrik wanted to spend more time with Mattie, even if it was just the short trip back home. But once he got there, he'd have nothing to do for the rest of the afternoon, except homework. It wouldn't hurt to get started on the research paper with Dawdi.

"That would be fine, if you have paper and a pen I can borrow," Henrik agreed.

"Good. Mattie, if you don't mind, why don't you stop and tell Bo and Skye to come over for supper, and then they can take Henrik home."

"Sure, I can do that. Thank you so much for the wonderful ride. I was so happy to meet you," she said, reaching out to shake Dawdi's hand.

"I'm happy to meet you too. I hope to see you again."

"Maybe I'll come to your farm sale."

"You do that."

Dawdi went into the house and Henrik walked Mattie to her car. The temptation to kiss her good-bye was strong, but he knew this wasn't the time or place. He would wait, but not much longer.

"Thank you for inviting me, Henrik," Mattie said, opening her car door. "Sorry I have to leave, but I really had fun. Maybe we can do something again sometime."

"Sounds good to me."

"See you in church tomorrow."

"Yeah. See you tomorrow."

Mattie slid behind the wheel and Henrik closed the door. He

watched as she turned the little Dodge around and drove out of the yard. His friends in Sweden would laugh long and loud if they knew he liked a girl whose parting words were, "See you in church tomorrow." They'd wonder what happened to him. He was starting to wonder too.

Henrik walked into the plain white Amish farmhouse. Grandma was in the kitchen, taking a pan of huge cookies out of the gas-powered oven. The smell was enough to make his stomach rumble and his mouth water. Nobody could beat Grandma's cooking.

"Let me guess. You smelled the cookies," the little woman with the bright brown eyes smiled up at him.

"Actually, it was Dawdi's idea," Henrik replied defensively.

"Ah yes, that doesn't surprise me. He's in the living room in his recliner."

Dawdi was lying motionless in his chair when Henrik walked into the room. His heart skipped a beat and he remembered worrying about Dawdi when they left on the buggy ride, but he'd seemed okay after that.

"Dawdi?"

The old man jerked awake, and opened his eyes. "Oh, Henrik. Sorry. I missed my nap today, so I was a bit tired."

"I'm sorry I woke you. I was worried that—" He couldn't say "that you were dead." What a terrible thing to say!

"—That you weren't feeling well."

"Don't you worry about me, young man. You have enough worries of your own, like a research paper, and having a good year in America, and a young lady," Dawdi chuckled softly as he leaned forward in his recliner. "Did Grandma fix you up with some cookies?"

"Not yet."

"Then go get some for both of us and we'll talk."

Henrik returned with a heaping plate of large, soft cookies.

The Amish called them church cookies because they were passed around during the long worship services to help the children pass the time. They tasted even better than they smelled, he thought, biting into one.

"You want to know about people and places and how things have changed," Dawdi said, reaching for a cookie. "But before that, I want to tell you about choices.

"You probably think we Amish don't have a lot of choices. We dress alike, we have strict church traditions, and we don't go to school past eighth grade. That takes away a lot of the choices other people have to make.

"But we make choices too. We decide if we are going to stay Amish. Most people who are born Amish, stay Amish, so I guess you might say there isn't really a choice. But there is. We don't tie our children to the hitching post and make them be Amish. Our tradition is very strong so most of them stay, but they are not forced to. Does that make sense?"

Henrik nodded.

"We choose who we are going to marry. Some people think the Amish have arranged marriages. Not at all. We choose our spouses. That's one of the biggest decisions anybody makes, don't you think?"

Henrik nodded again.

"When I was your age and running around with the young folks, some of the kids smoked. Some quit, and some are still smoking. One of them—Abe Miller—he died just a month ago of lung cancer. It got him. We're all gonna die, Henrik, but smoking is one way to invite the death angel to come early."

Henrik shifted uneasily in his chair and took another cookie. Did Dawdi know he smoked? Did Bo tell him?

"Drinking—that was another thing we did when we were your age. It hurts and kills people too. Another choice you get to make. You made a big decision when you decided to come to

America. Now that you're here, you're getting to choose whether you'll have a good time. Are you having a good time?"

"Sure."

"Good. Make the right choices and you will."

Dawdi took his second cookie and chewed on it awhile before he continued. "The way I see history, Henrik, is choices. The decision of my ancestors to come to America. Their decision to settle in Pennsylvania, and then later for groups of people to move to Kansas. The decision to keep going and not give up, even when weather and disease and insects seemed too much to bear. The choice to trust in God and keep going in good times and bad.

"Maybe you think that the choices you make aren't as important or as far-reaching as those, but they are, Henrik. What you do with your life can be a blessing or a curse. When people walk past your casket at your funeral, what will they think? What will they say about you?"

Henrik didn't answer. He didn't like this talk. What was with the old man anyway?

Dawdi chewed thoughtfully on his cookie, his white beard moving up and down, up and down.

"It'll be up to you what they think and say. It will also be up to you and God what happens when you die. You know that, don't you?"

Henrik nodded, but only because it was the right thing to do.

"That's another choice you get to make—whether you are going to take the Lord as your savior."

Henrik was beginning to regret accepting Dawdi's invitation to stay and talk. He'd wanted to talk about history, not religion!

Dawdi leaned back in his recliner and stared out the window. The only sound in the house was the ticking of the clock. Henrik wondered where Grandma had gone, and wished desperately she'd come "interrupt" them.

"I guess the preacher in me got carried away," Dawdi said, looking intensely at Henrik. "Like I said, history is choices. Now if you want to know more about choices we made along the way—the kind your history teacher would like to know about—we could talk about when the Amish and other pacifist groups went to Washington to ask Congress for an alternative to fighting in the military. Or we can talk about how we got the law passed so our children can quit school after grade eight. Is that more what you had in mind?"

Henrik heaved a sigh of relief. Yes, that was definitely more what he had in mind.

FOURTEEN

SOMEONE POUNDING on his door woke Henrik the next morning. He knew it was Sunday and he had to get up for church. "Okay, okay! I'm up!" he called.

"Henrik, may I come in?" asked Skye. Her voice quivered and she sounded strange.

"Sure," he answered, sitting up in bed.

Skye stepped into the room. Henrik looked at her face and knew something was terribly wrong.

"Henrik. Dawdi—my Dawdi—he died. Early this morning."

Her voice broke and tears streamed down her face. Henrik tried to comprehend her words. Dawdi dead? No, he couldn't be!

Skye came and sat on his bed, her sobs filling the room. Henrik felt the hurt begin in his heart. It moved up to his throat and left a lump he could hardly swallow. He sat next to Skye and put his arm around her, not knowing what to say. He could only see Dawdi the day before—hitching up the horse, rubbing his chest and complaining of indigestion, then talking and acting fine during the ride. He remembered the scare he'd had when he saw Dawdi asleep in the recliner, his long white beard resting on his chest. But Dawdi had said he was just tired! He could see Dawdi eating church cookies and talking to him about choices. He could see him waving goodbye to him, and Bo and Skye as they left the yard last night just—Henrik looked at the clock—nine hours ago!

Skye's tears subsided and her sobs grew quiet. She wiped her eyes and blew her nose into a faded red bandanna, then, staring at the old handkerchief in her hands, she told Henrik what had happened.

"Dawdi woke Grandma up around five o'clock this morning and told her he wasn't feeling good. He had chest pains. He said it was his time to go. Grandma held him close. He said he loved her, closed his eyes, and he was gone."

"I can't believe it," Henrik spoke around the lump in his throat.

"Grandma sat with him. She knew I'd be walking past their place this morning. I wondered why Dawdi wasn't sitting out on the porch like he is every day when I walk by. Grandma came out and told me. I went in to see him. He looked so peaceful."

Skye gave in to another flood of tears, and Henrik could no longer hold back his own. He couldn't remember the last time he'd cried, or if he'd ever felt such sadness.

Henrik had never felt the emptiness that comes with the death of a loved one, and he was unprepared for the emotions that Dawdi's death evoked in him and in those around him.

He went with Bo and Skye to be with Grandma and the rest of the family. He'd never witnessed such grief. Each person's face—from Grandma, who'd lost her husband and best friend of 60 years, to the youngest grandchild—reflected a deep inner sadness. Henrik felt his own heart tearing with each reminder of Dawdi.

He walked around the farm, needing to be alone. He came to the place where he and Dawdi had worked together, moving things into place for the sale. He wondered if they would still have it. Hearing a horse whinny, he looked up and saw Sailor in the corral calling to the other horses that were hitched to buggies lined up along the fence. Poor Sailor—did he know? How would he understand that his master of so many years was gone?

Henrik walked over to a gate that led from the corral into the pasture. Sailor followed him, hoping to be let out. "No, Sailor," Henrik said softly, slipping through the gate and latching it behind him. He followed a well-worn path through the prairie grass, not knowing where it would take him, only that it led away from the heaviness that hung over the farmyard.

The rain that had threatened during yesterday's buggy ride hadn't fallen. Now, trudging along the path lined with tall grass, Henrik felt a few drops. He probably should go back, he thought, but he didn't turn around. He had to focus his attention on something other than the tragic events of the last few hours. He needed to find out where the trail led.

He soon came upon two enormous red-gold horses grazing side by side near a tree-lined creek. He watched them for awhile, and he could hear Dawdi saying, "The hardest thing will be my team of work horses. We've spent many hours together."

You don't have to worry about saying goodbye to your horses, Dawdi, Henrik thought. You left before they did.

Salty tears mingled with fresh raindrops and ran down Henrik's cheeks as he followed the trail. He had to find the end.

A hundred yards ahead, the path disappeared into a grove of trees lining the bank of a small creek. Horse droppings were scattered about on the hard-packed earth beneath the trees. The thick canopy overhead provided the horses with shade on a hot summer day, shelter from the rain and a break from the cold winter winds.

Henrik noticed something unusual in one of the trees and walked toward it for a closer look. The tree was a cottonwood, so large he couldn't reach all the way around it. Nailed to the tree were strips of wood forming a makeshift ladder to a platform ten feet above the ground. A wooden railing surrounded the platform. A tree house. Dawdi, or one of his kids, must have built a tree house here years ago. Henrik looked to see if the trail continued on past the trees, but it appeared to end at the creek. The trail that brought horses here for protection from the elements of nature had also brought children here to play.

A flash of color through the trees caught Henrik's attention. After a moment, Henrik recognized Bo and Skye. He waited for them to join him.

"We needed to get away for a while," Bo said as they approached. "You too?"

Henrik nodded. "This is a pretty cool place."

"I know." Skye said. "Angela and I spent a lot of time out here when we'd visit Dawdi and Grandma each summer. Dawdi built the tree house for us."

"Really? I wondered who built it."

"I remember one summer we came out here to the creek, and we had a mud fight. Angela, Dawdi and me. We all threw mud at each other until we were covered with it. I don't think Grandma believed her eyes when we showed up at the house."

"Dawdi was in on it too?"

"Yep. He was the most incredible grandfather a kid could ever want. He was funny and kind and wise, and loving and understanding. And when I grew up, I needed him as much as I did when I was young," Skye paused and pulled a faded red bandanna out of her pocket. Her voice trembled as she continued; "Do you know the story behind this?"

Henrik shook his head.

"One summer, when Angela and I were here, we got into a fight over a harmonica. She could play it and I couldn't, and that made me mad. So I threw hers in the outhouse. That evening, Dawdi and Grandma talked to me about what had happened. I started crying because I was sorry for what I'd done. That's when Dawdi gave me this bandanna. He told me to keep it because there would be other times in my life when I'd have to cry, and I'd need it. Then he said, 'Remember that Dawdi and Grandma love you, and God loves you even more.' " Skye burst into tears and wept in Bo's arms.

Henrik moved toward his host parents and put his arms around them both. Together they cried, each lost in their own memories of the man who'd touched their lives in so many ways.

Death, funerals and the helpless feeling of grief were all new to Henrik. There were times, during the next few days, when he felt like a stranger being forced to participate in a ritual he neither understood nor appreciated. If that force had come from people, he might have rebelled. But he was being drawn by his own emotions and his growing love for the man who had so suddenly left this earth and his family and friends.

Even more confusing were the different beliefs about what happened to Dawdi after he died. Henrik's upbringing told him that Dawdi's life was over. He'd been a good man, and now he was gone. Bo and Skye had another approach, which they talked about for a long time that Sunday evening. They believed that a person who was a Christian—"saved" was the word they used—would go to be with God. Dawdi's life on earth moved on to life with God. Skye talked about Dawdi being with Angela now, and how much fun that reunion must be.

The Amish had still another approach. Henrik went to the three-hour funeral service on Tuesday, but he couldn't understand the preachers, who spoke in Pennsylvania Dutch. He'd asked Skye what they'd said, but she didn't know either. What she did know was the Amish "hoped for eternal life, but there are no guarantees until judgment day." Henrik's background told him one thing, while in his heart he wished desperately that Dawdi was in heaven with God and Angela.

He tried to recall what Dawdi had said the day before he died, when he gave the "religion speech" that had frustrated Henrik so much at the time. He'd said something about using your life as a blessing or curse, and what people might say when they walked past his casket. Had Dawdi known people would be walking by his casket just three days later?

He'd also said that what happened when he died would be up to him and God. And he'd said something about taking the Lord as his savior—whatever that meant.

Dawdi was a good man, and he seemed to have a great relationship with God, Henrik concluded. If anybody could get to heaven, Dawdi could.

Henrik had missed two days of school, and he was glad to see Mattie when she stopped by Tuesday evening. He needed her warmth, her smile and the assurance that these sad days would eventually come to an end. He waited for her on the porch. She came up the steps and reached out to hold him in a silent embrace. Henrik had hugged more people in the last few days than he had in his entire life, but this one felt especially good.

"I'm so sorry," she said, her face against his chest. "I can't imagine how you must feel. You knew him much better than I did."

"I felt like I was just getting to know him," he answered quietly.

Mattie pulled away and looked up at Henrik. "Did you go to the funeral?"

"Yeah. It was really long, and I didn't understand a word."

"I can imagine. Where was it? Were there a lot of people?"

"They had it in the biggest barn they could find in the community because they knew there would be a lot of people. They even came from other states. Dawdi was a very well known and respected man among the Amish. I've never seen so many buggies in one place in my life!"

"I'm so glad we went on that buggy ride together," Mattie said, sitting down on the porch step. "I liked the ride, but I liked talking to Dawdi just as much."

"I was really looking forward to interviewing him for my research paper," said Henrik, sitting down beside Mattie. "I don't know what I'm going to do now."

"Didn't you talk on Saturday after I left?"

"Yeah, but not about what I thought should go in the paper."

"What do you mean?"

"Oh, he talked a lot about choices and religion—stuff like that."

"Tell me about it."

The sun dropped over the horizon as Henrik began to recount his discussion with Dawdi. Zeb came and laid on the porch behind them, dusk turned to darkness, and still Henrik and Mattie talked. Never before had Henrik talked so long and so intensely with someone about such deep issues. Finally Mattie said she had homework to do, and had to leave.

Henrik walked her to her car. This time, when he drew her close, she came willingly. And when he bent down to kiss her, her lips met his.

FIFTEEN

THE MORNING of the Bontrager auction dawned clear and beautiful. Henrik was there at sunrise, helping family members carry household sale items out to the lawn. He paused for a moment, listening to the birds singing their welcome to the sun creeping above the horizon, and wondered if Dawdi was somewhere watching the final preparations for his farm sale. Three weeks ago, before Dawdi died, and before Henrik had spent hours talking to Mattie about life and death, that notion would never have crossed his mind. Now he found it interesting to think that if Dawdi had gone to be with God, he might be looking down at those he'd left behind.

He walked toward the house and met Mattie on her way outside with a box full of dishes. "Hey Mattie," he grinned, happy that she'd agreed to spend the day with him and help with the sale. "Do you think Dawdi is someplace watching us today?"

"Could be, but I doubt it," she said, returning his smile. "I think he has better things to do with his eternal life than watch a farm auction."

"Like what?"

"Like being in the presence of God. That's gotta be more rewarding than watching people bid on this box of old dishes," Mattie's dark eyes danced as she looked up at Henrik.

"You think?" Henrik teased.

"Without a doubt."

"How do you know? You haven't been there."

"In the presence of God? Well, not actually looking at God, no. But I've felt God's presence."

"When?"

"This box is getting heavy, Henrik. As much as I'd like to have a deep, theological discussion with you, could we maybe postpone it just a bit?"

Henrik grinned and reached for the dishes. "Let me take that heavy box, and you can walk with me while we have our heavy talk. What do you think will happen to these dishes when they die? Will they go to heaven?"

"Oh Henrik, don't make fun."

"Maybe it's more like this," Henrik placed the box on a table and took out one of the dishes. "This plate will be purchased today and go to a new life someplace else. It won't die. It'll just start over in a new setting. Maybe that's what happens to people. We move on to another setting—or another being. You know what I mean?"

"I know exactly what you mean," Mattie responded, taking the plate from Henrik's hand. "But we're not talking reincarnation. We're talking redemption. This plate—you and I— were purchased by Jesus so that we can, indeed, begin a new life some place else when we die. Yes, we'll start over in a new setting—a much better setting than we can imagine. Yes, we'll be another being—a being with God. You know what I mean?"

"I haven't a clue," Henrik teased. "But you can take as long as you want to teach me." He leaned close to Mattie, his eyes searching hers. "I'm all yours."

"And I'm all busy helping with the sale," Mattie said, picking up the box. "How about you?"

"Oh yes, me too." Henrik turned and walked quickly toward the house. "Definitely. Me too," he called back over his shoulder.

He smiled to himself as carried out another armload of sale items. He enjoyed talking with Mattie about God stuff. It was interesting, and obviously Mattie liked talking with him about those things. He wanted to pursue anything she enjoyed doing with him. Besides, she didn't get angry when he teased her about her "religion addiction." She just said it was an addiction she could live with, and he ought to try it. Yeah, right.

Cars, trucks and buggies began arriving an hour before the 10 o'clock sale. The leaves on the large cottonwood trees shone golden in the morning sun, and tinkled like a huge wind chime in the soft breeze. It was a perfect day for a farm auction.

When Dawdi died, the family had considered postponing the auction. It would be especially difficult for Grandma to see a lifetime of accumulated earthly possessions on the auction block so soon after losing her husband. But since the sale bills had already been distributed in Kansas as well as Amish communities in other states, they decided to continue as planned.

"Grandma will be okay," Skye assured Bo and Henrik. "She has her family and God to lean on. It will be hard, but she'll be okay."

Henrik watched Grandma closely that day as the auctioneer chattered his way around the farmyard. She was dressed in black mourning clothes, from her bonnet to her shoes. Her family and friends, many of who were also dressed in black, surrounded her with love and support, rarely leaving her side.

Henrik recalled what Grandma had said to him the evening before the funeral. Even now, he had trouble comprehending the thoughtfulness of the old Amish woman.

He, along with Bo and several Amish men, had been "sitting with the body." It was an Amish tradition that someone remain with the body at all times until the burial, so men of the church and family took turns keeping vigil. Henrik had been reluctant to accept Bo's invitation to join him "for the experience." Sitting with a dead body for several hours didn't seem like a very cool thing to do. But this would also be Bo's first time to participate in the tradition, and he'd almost insisted that Henrik come along.

At first he felt intimidated by the three Amish men sitting in the room, wearing their plain, unadorned clothes and looking so solemn and serious. It was strange to see Dawdi's body in the homemade coffin, looking almost like he had when he was napping in the recliner. Henrik kept expecting to see his chest move up and down with a breath, but it was ever so still.

Henrik's uneasiness soon disappeared. The Amish men began talking about Dawdi, telling stories of what they'd done with him, his teenager adventures, his family and his life in the Amish community. Just like Dawdi, the stories were full of life, laughter, and wisdom.

At one point, Henrik volunteered his own experiences with Dawdi, mentioning his intent to write a research paper about him. Grandma had apparently been listening in the next room, because after Henrik finished talking she came and put her small, warm hand on his shoulder, and said quietly, "Henrik, if I can help you with your paper, now that Dawdi is gone, let me know."

Her generous offer, in the midst of her grief, was completely unexpected. Henrik didn't know what to say, except "Thank you."

Henrik returned his attention to the sale. It was fun to listen to the auctioneer, although sometimes it was hard to understand his fast auctioneer-talk. Right now, he was holding up some woodworking tools. "These tools have some wear on them, but they have a lot more left," the auctioneer said. "I'll take a ten dollar bill."

Wood tools. Dawdi's wood tools. Something clicked inside of Henrik. "Yes!" he shouted, then recoiled at his own voice. He flushed as everyone in the crowd turned to stare at him.

"I'm bid 10, would you give me 15," the auctioneer chanted.

A young Amish man raised his hand.

"I've got 15, now give me 20...20...20..." Henrik raised his hand.

"I've got 20, now 25." The Amish man nodded.

"Twenty-five, now 30." Henrik nodded.

"Thirty, now 35." The Amish man hesitated, looked at Henrik, and nodded.

The crowd looked at Henrik. The auctioneer held the tools toward him.

"Will you give me 40, young man?" Henrik nodded. Caught up in the spirit of the bidding, he'd gone this far. He wouldn't quit now.

The attention turned toward Henrik's bidding opponent as the auctioneer asked him for $45. The man declined, shaking his head.

"Forty-five dollars for these fine wood-working tools! Anybody in at 45?"

Silence. Henrik's heart was beating so hard he was sure Mattie, standing next to him, could hear it.

"Sold to the young man over here for $40!" They handed the tools to Henrik, and he accepted them almost reverently. Wouldn't his dad be shocked to see him now?

The sale continued well into the afternoon. The auctioneer led the crowd briskly through rows of household goods, furniture, clothes, horse tack, livestock supplies and equipment, tools, fencing material, farming implements, and miscellaneous items that had accumulated through the years. Hand-in-hand, Henrik and Mattie moved with the crowd. Mattie bought a few things, but Henrik's purchases ended with the tools.

By four o-clock the auctioneer was nearing the end of the last row of farm equipment. Henrik knew the last thing to be sold would be the team of Belgian horses.

A few people had already gathered around the corral and

were admiring the huge horses while they waited for the auctioneer. Henrik and Mattie joined Bo and Skye standing next to the fence.

"Are there some good buyers here?" Henrik asked.

"I think so. I've seen a couple of Amish men looking at them, but there are some here that I don't know," Skye answered.

"Will they sell as a team?" Mattie wondered.

"Depends on the buyer. If the auctioneer gets a buyer that wants just one, he'll split them up."

"That would be terrible," Mattie sighed.

"It'd break their hearts, I think, after all these years," Bo added.

The crowd grew as the auctioneer approached the gate leading into the horse corral. Grandma was there, flanked by her son, E.J., her son-in-law, Caleb, and a number of other family members.

"Gonna sell the Belgians," the auctioneer called out. "They're 15-year-old geldings, sound and safe, a beautiful matched pair. Money times two for the team, or take your pick."

The auctioneer began his chant at $1,000. When nobody picked up the bid, he stopped and said, "Ladies and gentlemen, you won't find a nicer pair of draft horses in the county. They know how to work, they've been well cared for, and they have many years left in them. Who'll give me $700?"

An Amish man standing next to the corral nodded his head, and the bidding was on its way. A second Amish man and two "English outsiders" contested for the bid. The Amish men dropped out when it reached $1,200, and at $1,500 one of the remaining two men shook his head.

"I've got $1,500—your pick or times two for the team. Do I hear 16?" Silence.

"Sold for $1,500. You want both?"

"No. I'll take the one without the socks."

Henrik heard a muffled gasp beside him, and turned to see

Skye shaking her head.

"He can't do that," she said. "He can't split them up. They've been together since they were colts, playing in the pasture."

"Gonna sell the other Belgian," the auctioneer continued. "He's worth the same money. I'm bid a thousand, who'll give me eleven hundred?"

The outsider who'd lost the bid on the first horse nodded his head.

"Eleven, I have 11—who'll give me 12? I've got 12," the auctioneer chanted, looking at someone near Henrik. Henrik turned to see who was bidding. He couldn't tell.

"Twelve, now 13." The outsider nodded.

"Thirteen, now 14."

Henrik turned again, looking for the bidder, and saw Skye nod her head at the auctioneer. She was bidding on the horse!

"Fourteen, now 15...15...15!" The man shook his head. "I've got 14—anybody give me 15?" Silence.

"Sold to the lady for $1,400."

Henrik turned to speak to Skye, but she was already walking straight toward the man who had bought the first horse. Bo, caught by surprise, went after her. Henrik grabbed Mattie's hand and followed.

"...can't separate the team," he heard her say to the first buyer.

"I just want one—I don't need both," the man replied, crossing his arms defensively.

"I'd like to buy him back from you. Will you take $1,600?"

"No, I don't think so." The man moved away.

"Sir!" Skye called firmly. The man stopped and turned back. "Sir, what will you take for that horse?"

Henrik, Mattie and Bo watched as the man's eyes studied Skye. He looked at the horses in the corral, then back at Skye.

"Three thousand."

Henrik looked at Mattie and Bo, his eyebrows raised in surprise.

"Will you take a check?" he heard Skye ask, hardly believing his ears.

"Sure."

Bo looked stunned, but Skye didn't miss a beat. She took out her checkbook, wrote a check and handed it to the man. She shook his hand, and then turned to the trio behind her.

"Did you say she could do that?" Henrik asked Bo.

"I didn't have to. My wife's singing career made her wealthy, and if she wants to spend $4,400 for a pair of horses that we have no use for, then that's up to her," Bo replied. "In case you haven't noticed, Skye has both a mind and money of her own."

SIXTEEN

ZEB WAS CONFUSED and frustrated. Two enormous four-legged creatures were grazing in the pasture with his sheep. They looked and smelled like the horses that occasionally brought visitors to the farm, but they were much larger. Reebok, the llama that protected the flock from predators, didn't seem worried, but the Border Collie didn't like having strange creatures in his pasture with his sheep. Barking was the only way Zeb knew to tell Bo and Skye that something was wrong, and maybe scare the big critters away. But several hours of non-stop barking failed to bring Bo or Skye, and the Belgian horses paid no attention to the noisy black and white dog.

Bo was working late at the motorcycle shop in Vicksburg, Skye was doing a concert at a banquet near Vicksburg, and Henrik was home with Mattie. They'd fallen into the comfortable habit of her bringing him home after school. They'd share an after-school snack, talk and hang out for awhile. Then they either studied together or Mattie would go home. Tonight they were working on American History, but Zeb's incessant barking made it impossible for Henrik to concentrate.

"Stupid dog!" he blurted, standing up abruptly from the dining room table. Striding to the back door, he flung it open and yelled, "ZEB! SHUT UP! JUST SHUT UP!"

"Maybe we should go see what he's barking at," Mattie suggested.

"I know what he's barking at. It's just Skye's horses."

"Why is he barking at them?"

"Because he's stupid, that's why."

"I thought Border Collies were supposed to be smart dogs," Mattie said, joining Henrik at the door.

"Zeb used to be smart. Now he's stupid," Henrik stepped out onto the porch.

"Is he barking at them because they're new and he doesn't think they belong here?"

"Heck if I know. I'm not a dog psychologist," Henrik headed down the steps and out to the yard where he could see Zeb, sitting on his haunches near the fence, his black and white face raised toward the dark sky.

"Zeb!" Henrik hollered as he approached the dog. "The horses aren't hurting you. Get used to it!"

Zeb stood and walked toward Henrik, wagging his tail as if in apology. He would gladly trade barking for a little attention.

"See, you just had to explain it to him," Mattie said, coming to stand next to Henrik and slipping her hand in his. "I know somebody else who took some time to get used to a new situation."

"What do you mean?"

"Oh, you know. At the beginning you thought being here was going to hurt you. You barked a lot."

"I did?"

"You did." Mattie shivered. "It's cold out here. Can we go back inside?"

Henrik bent down and scratched Zeb's ears with his free hand. "No more barking, Zeb. Understand?"

Henrik and Mattie ran hand-in-hand toward the house, and Zeb followed them up onto the porch. They closed the door behind them. Moments later, the barking began again.

"I guess he doesn't learn as fast as you did," Mattie laughed.

"Exactly what are you getting at? What's this about me barking and learning fast?"

"You know, Henrik, when you came here you had an attitude. Like when you thought I owed you a date if you kicked that field goal. You thought you were God's gift to women."

"Excuse me? I didn't even think about God, so how could I think I was God's gift to women?"

"It's just an expression. Anyway, you thought you were cool and could get away with things like smoking."

"What makes you think that?"

"I could smell it."

Henrik went to the refrigerator and took out a can of Dr. Pepper. "Want something to drink?"

"Water's fine."

Henrik filled a glass of water, set it on the table by Mattie, and sat down beside her.

"Sounds like you think you have me all figured out."

"Not completely. But I do know you've changed since you came three months ago."

"How?"

"You came with an attitude. You made it obvious that you thought life in Sweden was much better than it is here. You acted like you tolerated Kansas people, our rules, our school, our church because you had no choice. You—"

"Hey! Give me a break! When did I say I didn't like it here?"

"You didn't have to say it in so many words. We got the idea."

Henrik took a drink of Dr. Pepper and then sat staring at the can for a long time.

"When did it change?"

"Don't you know?"

"Not really."

"I'm not exactly sure why or how you changed, but I noticed

it when you started treating me like something more than an object to be conquered. When we could talk and joke around as friends—that's when I began to see that you could be fun. Like the night of the video scavenger hunt."

"Sometimes I still can't believe I wore that woman's clothes and perfume," Henrik laughed.

"You stopped acting like the world owed you something and just enjoyed being silly like the rest of us."

"Man, you're really getting on my case here," Henrik faked a scowl. "Was I really that bad?"

Mattie reached for Henrik's can of Dr. Pepper and held it up. "I'm not going to call you bad, but here's another example. When you came, you couldn't understand how a group of kids could have a great time without drinking and smoking, and you didn't understand why you weren't supposed to do that here. Am I right?"

Henrik took the can back from Mattie. "What's with the past tense? Do you think, if I had a choice, I would rather be sitting here right now with a Dr. Pepper than with a beer?" He grinned. "Dream on, girl."

"I'm not totally dense," Mattie smiled. "I know you haven't given it up permanently. But you do have a choice right now, because I bet Bo has a beer or two in this house. And you had a choice about smoking. It seems to me you've made right choices lately because you want to be here, and you're willing to give up some things that you thought were very important so you can stay."

"That Zeb better give up his barking if he wants to stay alive," Henrik said, standing up and walking to the door. He opened it and stared at the dog near the fence.

"Give him time. He'll get used to the horses, and realize they belong here," said Mattie, following him to the door.

"I'll tell you what I'm getting used to," Henrik said, wrapping his arms around Mattie. "You belonging here," he held her close. "You know what I mean?"

"Yes," she said softly.

He'd wanted her to spend the night. If Mattie had been a girl back home, he would have asked her to stay. It would have been expected at this point in their relationship. But Henrik knew Mattie would never have agreed. Her strong religious beliefs wouldn't have allowed it to happen. Still, he could feel the fire smoldering inside her. Later, getting ready for bed, he wondered how long it would take before it burst into flame. Mattie wasn't an angel, after all. She was a teenager with desires just like his. The only difference was, she hadn't given in to those desires.

Well it was time she did, and he would be the man to show her how. Henrik smiled as he turned off the light and crawled into bed. Talking was all fine and good, but there comes a time when words aren't enough. There comes a time when passion and desires must be fulfilled. He would ignite that fire within her. Oh yes, he would.

Nothing changed during the next month. They talked, held hands and shared sweet, lingering kisses. Henrik ached for more, but Mattie would go no further.

His research paper on Grandma Bontrager was due the Monday following Thanksgiving, and Henrik made a deal with Mattie. If he finished the project by Sunday evening, they would celebrate with dinner at a nice restaurant—-his treat, if she would drive.

Henrik sat at Skye's desk and typed the last paragraph midway through Sunday afternoon. Bo was watching a football game in the family room, and Skye was performing a concert at the Vicksburg mall to raise money for the Children's Christmas Tree Fund.

"It's done!" Henrik announced, entering the family room. "Now I can celebrate with Mattie."

"Where are you guys going?" Bo asked, his eyes on the television screen.

"I don't know. I told her to pick a nice place," Henrik flopped onto the couch.

"Gonna cost you a lot of money."

"It'll be worth it."

"Yeah, she's a sweet girl."

"Bo, what do women want?"

Bo's eyes left the game momentarily. "What do you mean?"

"You know. What turns them on? Mattie's sweet and everything, but I can't get beyond the passes with her. No touchdowns, if you know what I mean."

Bo grinned. "Women want talk, affection, romance. That kind of thing."

"I've done all that."

"And?"

"And she seems to love it. But that's as far as I can get."

"Henrik," Bo chuckled, "You are dating a young woman with some mighty strong moral standards. It's as simple as that."

"You mean her religion is more important to her than I am?"

"I wouldn't presume to say what's most important to Mattie. You'll have to find that out from her."

Maybe I have, Henrik thought unhappily. "What about you and Skye?"

"What about us?"

"She was a rock star when you guys met. She couldn't have been Miss Perfect."

"Oh no, she was far from that."

"So you guys slept together before you got married?"

Bo gave him a strange look, and Henrik regretted asking the question. It was really none of his business.

"Actually, no."

The answer surprised Henrik. "No? Why not?"

"Because we didn't get serious about each other until after Angela died and Skye had become a Christian."

"She got religion and there went your hopes," Henrik smirked.

Bo leaned toward Henrik. "Actually, when Skye and I got hooked up with God, we had more hope than we'd ever had before."

It was Henrik's turn to stare at the football game. Obviously he wasn't going to get any help from Bo. It didn't matter, anyway. He could handle Mattie quite fine by himself.

SEVENTEEN

HENRIK COULDN'T IMAGINE a guy showing more sensitivity, or being more romantic, or looking any better than he did that evening on his date with Mattie. Even Bo commented on his appearance, and Mattie said he smelled good, too.

Mattie looked especially beautiful. Her dark, shoulder-length hair was piled on top of her head with tiny ringlets falling across her forehead. She seldom wore make-up, but tonight her brown eyes sparkled more than usual, which Henrik attributed partly to her being in love, and partly to eye make-up. A light application of soft, rosy blush highlighted her cheekbones and lipstick enhanced her beautiful smile. She wore a short, red velvet dress with a neckline just low enough to show off a ruby necklace. Henrik admired Mattie's long legs, but wished the dress hadn't been so modest.

They enjoyed a wonderful meal in an Italian restaurant, talking about his family in Sweden, her family, school and their friends. Listening to her and looking across the table at her in the soft light of the restaurant, Henrik yearned for what he hoped would come later in the evening.

They parked along a country road near Wellsford, and Henrik wasted no time claiming the lips he'd been admiring all evening. Her kisses were warm and welcoming. He knew she wanted more. His hand caressed her neck, finding the ruby necklace. Slowly his hand moved down, searching, hoping. She stopped him, just as she had every other time. But tonight Henrik wasn't giving up without a fight. He told her that if they loved each other, it should be okay. He challenged her, saying he was beginning to doubt her love for him. Mattie cried, and could only answer, "I don't want to go any farther. Please understand."

He didn't understand. She drove him home and dropped him off without even a goodnight kiss. He watched her tail lights disappear in the dark November night, then paced up and down the lane between the house and the road. He needed a smoke. He searched his coat pockets, hoping to find a cigarette. Just one.

There was a note from Mattie in his school locker the next morning. He read it quickly, then stuffed it into the pocket of his jeans. Mattie avoided him all day, adding to his frustration. When school was out, he asked Winston to take him home.

"Why aren't you riding with Mattie?" Winston asked as they walked to his car.

"Little Miss Mattie thinks she's too good for me," Henrik growled.

"Since when?"

"Last night."

Winston and Henrik got into the car and threw their books into the back seat. Moments later they were on the road. The 55-mph speed limit sign passed in a blur as Henrik read 75 on the car's speedometer.

"So what happened last night?" Winston asked.

Henrik recounted the evening, then pulled out Mattie's note. "Today I get this letter:

Dear Henrik,
  I cried a lot last night after I got home. It hurt so bad to

disagree with you, especially after such a beautiful evening together. But I just can't—won't—give in to what you want to do together. I think we need to have an understanding— either we agree on the lines we are going to respect sexually, or we can't continue our relationship. We need to talk.

Love, Mattie.

Henrik stuck the note back in his pocket and looked at Winston. "What do you think?"

"I think she's a goody-goody, like I've told you all along."

"So what do I do?"

"Drop her. What's the point of staying with her?"

"She's fun. She's gorgeous."

"Doesn't sound like she's much fun on a date and 'gorgeous' isn't doing you a lot of good, is it?"

"Nope."

"Then kiss the chick good-bye."

Henrik didn't answer. He just stared out the window, feeling as drab and colorless as the late November landscape flying by.

"You want a smoke?" Winston offered.

He'd show prissy little Mattie he didn't need her. Let her keep her morals and uppity standards. He could have a lot more fun without her. He could hang out with Winston, Mitch and the other guys, and sneak a smoke when he wanted, The guys were more fun to talk to anyway. They discussed girls, not God.

Talking to Mattie was pointless, Henrik decided. He put a note in her locker saying he'd tried his best to show her a good time that Sunday evening, and if it wasn't good enough and he wasn't good enough for her, then so be it. Good-bye.

Word of their break-up traveled fast at Rolling Prairie High

School. Everyone seemed to know everyone else's business, accurate or not. Henrik hated being the topic of the latest juicy gossip, but he told the guys he didn't care. Winston knew the whole story and soon whispers of "why" had replaced "what."

Henrik was surprised by the reactions from the students. If this happened in Sweden, it would create a bit of conversation, then life would go on. But here he could tell whose side the kids were on just by passing them in the hallway.

There were the guys who joked with him and said, "You're the man, Henrik," and gave him the thumbs-up sign. There were also guys who said nothing—-the religious types like Mattie. There were girls who gave him nasty looks, like he was some kind of criminal. But there were also the girls who showed an obvious interest in dating him—-girls he'd never noticed when he was with Mattie. Well, he was noticing them now! Henrik smiled as he walked to History class that Friday. He was a free man this weekend, and he could hardly wait.

When Selena, a cute blond cheerleader who occasionally worked as a model in Vicksburg, invited him to a party at her house Saturday evening, Henrik immediately accepted. Her parents were away, and the party offered everything he'd missed in Kansas—alcohol, cigarettes, hard rock music, even marijuana. Henrik felt right at home.

"Gonna break some rules tonight, Swede?" Winston grinned and pulled two cans of beer out of the cooler in the garage.

"I don't think Selena invited my area rep," Henrik laughed. "Do you know how long it's been since I've had a beer?"

"Too darn long," Winston said, handing him a Coors.

Henrik figured if he stopped drinking midway through the evening, he would be reasonably sober by his 1:00 a.m. curfew. Bo and Skye would surely be in bed when he got home, so they'd never know. He'd be up and ready go to church with them in the morning.

When he started looking for a ride home, Selena surprised him by offering to take him. When they drove up to his house, she reminded him that she'd never been there before and would love to see inside.

"Maybe some other time," Henrik said. "We don't want to wake Bo and Skye."

"We'll be quiet," she whispered, putting her arm into his. "Please, oh please!"

Against his better judgment, he took her into the house. Holding his finger to his lips, Henrik flipped on the lights and gestured toward the kitchen and family room. "It's a cool house," he whispered, "but I can't give you the full tour."

"Okay," she mouthed. "But can I see your bedroom?"

Henrik led her across the house and opened his door. He closed it behind them, feeling a little safer. Selena admired his CD collection, then pulled one out and slipped it into the player.

"I love this song," she said, stretching out on his bed.

The sharp rapping on his door startled Henrik awake. His clock read 2:00 a.m. He'd fallen asleep, but worst of all, Selena was sleeping soundly beside him. Damn.

"Come in," he called. What else could he do? They knew she was there. Maybe it would help if they saw her fully clothed, crashed on top of the bed covers.

Bo opened the door and stood there silently for a moment.

"Curfew is 1:00 a.m., Henrik. And you know the house rules about girls in your room."

"Right," Henrik said, shaking Selena awake. "We just fell asleep listening to music."

"Right," Bo echoed, turning away.

Henrik walked Selena to her car, thanked her for the ride home, and hurried back to the house.

Church was the last place Henrik wanted to be the next morning. He tried to stay awake during Pastor Marge's sermon, but his eyes kept closing. Each time he'd tell himself, "Only for a moment." Then his head would nod and he'd wake up.

Bo and Skye had been unusually quiet that morning. He knew why, he thought drowsily. He was in trouble.

After church, they ate lunch at the Wellsford Pizza Hut. While they waited for their order, Bo asked Henrik what he thought of the sermon.

"I don't know. I had trouble concentrating today."

"It's one of the best Advent sermons I've ever heard," Skye remarked. "What do you do in Sweden for Advent?"

Henrik's foggy brain tried to remember. "We open calendars."

"Open calendars? What do you mean?" Skye leaned toward him.

"Calendars where you open a little door for each day of Advent."

"What's behind the little doors?"

"Pictures or candy. Different stuff."

"Sounds like fun. Do you think you'll miss your Christmas traditions this year?"

"No."

"How about your family?" Bo asked.

"No."

"You don't miss home at all, do you?"

"Not really."

"That's good," Bo said. "We're glad you're having a good time here. But if having a good time involves breaking curfew and having girls in your room—"

Their pizza arrived and Bo didn't finish his sentence until everyone had a piece on their plate. He took a bite, then continued, "If having a good time means choosing to ignore our house rules, then we're really hurt and disappointed. That kind of choice doesn't build a trusting relationship."

Henrik flinched. If they were hurt and disappointed at that, what would happen if they found out about the party?

EIGHTEEN

EVERY TIME the phone rang that day, Henrik was afraid it was someone calling to tell Bo and Skye about Selena's party. That evening there was a call for him.

"It's Kory," said Skye, handing him the phone. His area rep!

"Hello," said Henrik, his heart pounding.

"Hi, Henrik, how's it going?"

"Fine. Everything's great."

"I know you had a good football season. Are you going out for basketball?"

"Yeah. I don't know how much I'll get to play, but I'm on the team."

"That's good. What about your classes? Are you doing okay in history and government?"

"Yeah, I got an A on a research paper I wrote about Skye's Amish grandmother."

"Good for you, Henrik! I'd love to read it."

Let's get it over with, Henrik thought. If you called because Bo and Skye told you about Selena being in my room, just say so.

"What's your family doing for Christmas? Going any place?"

"I don't think so. Skye's parents are coming here from Pennsylvania."

"Well, you be sure to tell them about your Swedish traditions. And don't forget to do the 'Santa Lucia' for them. You know, wear the tall white hat and sing the song."

"You've gotta have a girl to be the Lucia."

Kory laughed. "Yeah, you're right. Maybe you can rent a Donald Duck movie and watch it on Christmas Day—that's a Swedish tradition you could share with your family."

"'Yeah, right."

"Sorry, I'm giving you a hard time," Kory laughed. "I just wanted to check in to see how things are going. Is there anything I need to know?"

"Nope, I'm doing fine."

"Then you have a good Christmas and I'll call again next year!"

"Sure. Talk to you later." Henrik turned off the cordless phone and uttered a huge sigh of relief.

Selena followed him like a puppy the next day in school, and once again Henrik found himself to be the main topic of conversation. Last week the focus of school gossip had been his breakup with Mattie. Now everyone was speculating on his relationship with Selena. Three days ago he'd been intrigued by her interest in him, but for some reason being linked with the sexy blond no longer appealed to him. She liked to party, she wasn't shy about showing off her great figure, and he was pretty sure she wouldn't make him stop after the first kiss. Still, there was something about her that just didn't click with him. Even more confusing was the feeling that, had he met her in Sweden, he would have responded much differently.

He wondered what Mattie would say when she saw him in American History. She'd probably ignore him, treat him like dirt. They broke up because he wanted more than she would give, and now he was linked to someone with a reputation of giving herself with few restraints. He'd never known Mattie to act mean toward anyone, but it might be interesting to see that side of her, even if he was the recipient.

He was the first one in the classroom. Mattie came in soon after and put her books on the desk next to his.

"Hi, Henrik. I have a question for you."

Here it comes, he thought. "What?" he asked.

"Our youth group is having a Christmas banquet, and I was wondering if you'd like to go with me," Mattie said, her dark eyes searching his face. "You know, as a friend."

Speechless, Henrik stared at her. A week ago he'd broken up with this girl. Surely she knew how angry he'd been. Today he was being paired with Selena, a girl who was entirely the opposite of Mattie. And now she was asking him to attend a banquet with her.

"Uh, I don't know," he stumbled. "When is it?"

"December 13. It's a Saturday evening. After the banquet, we go Christmas caroling. It's a lot of fun."

He wanted to ask why she was bothering with him, but there was no time. Class was about to begin.

"I'll let you know," he answered. "Thanks for asking."

She flashed him a smile, but all he could do was shake his head. He thought he knew this girl, but her invitation made no sense at all. He tore a piece of paper out of his notebook and scribbled, "If you can take me home today, we can talk about it."

He handed the note to Mattie. She read it, smiled and nodded.

Rolling Prairie was the perfect name for the sprawling brick school building set in a treeless expanse of grass. There was nothing to temper the onslaught of the cold north winds that buffeted the school and its students in the winter. That afternoon, as he and Mattie battled the wind across the parking lot to her car, Henrik wished for the calm cold of his home in Sweden. No wonder Kansas weather forecasters talked about the "wind chill factor." The temperature alone did not gauge the cold.

It took several miles for Mattie's car to heat up, and during that time they passed a horse and buggy on the road.

"I don't see how they do it," Mattie commented. "We're freezing in here waiting for the heater to warm up. They don't have any heaters at all."

"I don't know. I should ask Grandma about that."

"How's she doing?"

"She's okay. Her daughter's house is just a few steps away, and that helps a lot."

"You know what we should do?"

"What?"

"We should go caroling at her place."

"Yeah, that'd be cool."

"Are you coming along?"

"I don't know," Henrik paused.

"Why not?"

"Because I don't understand why you asked me to go to the banquet with you just a week after you wrote me that note."

Mattie was quiet. Henrik tried the heater fan to see if the air was warm. It was—barely.

"I wrote the note because I wanted to talk to you about our physical relationship. Then we never got to talk about it. You just wrote back and said it was over. I'd hoped we could come to a decision together, one way or the other."

"Mattie, have you never done anything with a guy?"

Mattie glanced quickly at Henrik, and a flush spread across her cheeks. "No more than with you."

"Haven't you ever wanted to?"

The flush deepened. "Yes."

"With me?"

"Yes."

"Then why not? Didn't we have something special between us?"

"I like you a lot Henrik. In fact, I think I was falling in love with you. I loved that feeling...going to sleep at night, dreaming about you. I'd never felt that way about a guy before."

"Then why...?"

"I've made a promise to myself and to God that I will save that part of myself for the man I marry. Too many girls and guys have sex and then there's nothing special left for the person they marry."

"But how will you know if you get along with each other sexually? Isn't that important?"

"It's very important. But if we are a good match in other areas, I think we'll be able to get along in bed too."

Henrik turned the heater fan on full blast and the car was soon warm. "So, you think I'm a bad guy?"

Mattie hesitated before answering. "I think you grew up in a different culture with different values than I did. I don't think you're bad. I do think it might be worth reconsidering some of your values and your relationship to God."

Henrik squirmed. "Is that why you asked me to the banquet? To try to convert me?"

"I asked you because I still like you, and I think the banquet and caroling would be a neat Christmas tradition for you to experience. You decide if you want to go."

"Sure, what the heck. I've got nothing better to do that evening."

"We got a call today from Bryan and Gale," Skye announced that evening during supper. "You know them, Bo. They have that pottery store in the little town of Miltown. They're having a Christmas open house every weekend this month, and they need some help. They were wondering if we wanted to come down the

13th and 14th."

"Sounds good to me, if Henrik wants to manage the farm," Bo said, reaching for the saltine crackers. He broke several into his bowl of chili, then looked up at Henrik. "What do you think? Are you interested, or do you have plans for that weekend?"

"Mattie invited me to a Christmas banquet and caroling," Henrik answered. "But I'll be around here."

"Drat, we'll miss the church Christmas banquet," Skye said. "That's always a treat. But I'd really like to help Bryan and Gale if we could."

"Can't be both places," Bo said, then paused as he looked at Henrik with a slight grin. "Did you say Mattie invited you to the banquet? How many women do you have on the string now? Selena and Mattie?"

Henrik blushed. "I don't have any on the string. I'm not dating either one of them."

"Okay, none of my business," Bo wiped his mouth with his napkin and looked at Henrik. Henrik knew he was laughing at him. He could see it spilling out of Bo's eyes.

Henrik tried to study for an English test later that evening, but he couldn't concentrate. After what happened last weekend, Bo and Skye were going to trust him again when they went to Miltown. Mattie wanted to take him to a Christmas banquet. Selena was practically throwing herself at him and he wasn't interested. What was going on, anyway?

NINETEEN

Henrik had never ignored the attentions of a pretty girl, but during the next week in school that's exactly what he did with Selena. He didn't know what, but something about her simply turned him off.

Just as confusing was his continued attraction to Mattie. He'd never been "just friends" with a girl, and Mattie's invitation to attend the Christmas banquet with her as a friend had both surprised and intrigued him. He missed the talks they'd had when they were dating, and that made no sense either. His relationships with girls had always been conversationally superficial and physically intense. So why was Mattie's friendship more important to him than Selena's offer of a good time without restrictions?

The question was still unanswered on the night of the banquet. He attended the dinner with Mattie and went caroling with the youth group. Singing Christmas songs in front of houses in the cold night air was a new experience for him, and not one his buddies in Sweden would consider a "good time." But Henrik found himself having fun. Even though he didn't know the songs very well, he loved watching Mattie, her face bright with the cold, her eyes sparkling as she sang of the long-ago birth of the Christ-child. He wanted to wrap his arms around her to keep her warm, to snuggle his chin on top of her head. But he couldn't. They were just friends now.

In Henrik's part of Sweden, winter meant snow on the ground. There was never a question about snow for Christmas. Kansans, Henrik found out, hoped for a white Christmas but often didn't get one.

Henrik woke up Christmas morning when something warm and furry slammed against him and a wet tongue lapped his face. He opened his eyes to see Zeb's black and white face. Bo stood in the doorway, laughing.

"Zeb wanted to say Merry Christmas, and come play in the snow."

"It's snowing?"

"Uh huh. I think it snowed most of the night. Maybe we can take the sleigh out today."

"You have a sleigh?" Henrik sat up and pushed Zeb aside.

"Caleb does. We'll all be at Grandma's for dinner, and after we open presents, maybe we can talk Caleb into hitching the horse up to the sleigh. Get up and come see a beautiful Christmas morning in Kansas."

Henrik smiled when he stepped out of the house a few minutes later. The ground was covered with several inches of brand new snow that sparkled in the morning sunlight. Across the yard, beside the small red barn, Skye's Belgian horses stood behind the white fence. Henrik whistled, and the horses' ears flipped forward. Beyond the horses, in front of the dark green pine trees, he saw Bo's sheep and their guard llama, Reebok, gathered around their hay feeder. It looks like an old-fashioned Kansas Christmas scene, Henrik mused.

Henrik saw more Christmas card scenes that day. Some he captured with his camera, and some he filed in his memory. There was Bo on his Harley, dressed like Santa Claus, heading down the lane toward Grandma's house. Santa Claus was not a part of Amish tradition, but that didn't stop Bo from enjoying the fun of playing the role for the kids.

There was Santa Bo giving the Amish children rides on his Harley, until Emma came to the door to tell them dinner was ready.

There was the unforgettable picture of Bo in his red Santa suit and long white beard carrying a small, slightly apprehensive Amish boy, his eyes huge with wonder, into the house.

There was the elderly Amish Grandma, her head bowed at the table, her white head covering speaking silently of her devotion. Around her, down both sides of the long tables, was her legacy of children and grandchildren, their heads also bowed in silent prayer. The long moments spoke to Henrik, and he wondered if the others were thinking what he was thinking. He missed Dawdi.

Later that afternoon, there was the scene of Caleb driving the horse and sleigh, making tracks in the fresh snow in a nearby field. The sleigh was piled so full of children, Henrik could hardly tell where one ended and the other began. When it was his turn to ride, Henrik held three Amish youngsters on his lap. Skye took a picture for him.

Then Bo decided to pull the kids on a sled tied to his motorcycle. It was hard to tell who was having more fun, Bo or the children. As the laughter and screams of delight drifted across the field, Henrik snapped pictures and wished for a video camera.

Later, as the pale yellow sun slipped down toward its winter bed, Henrik lifted the little boy named Kevin onto his shoulders and gave him a ride home to the farmyard. They talked about important things, like whether or not there was enough snow to make a snowman. Henrik wasn't sure, but Kevin was convinced there was. Henrik said it was getting dark, and Kevin said they could use a flashlight. Henrik finally promised to come back the next day to help him make a snowman, and Kevin was satisfied.

Early the next morning, Bo and Skye drove to Vicksburg to pick up her parents, who were flying in from Pennsylvania. When they returned several hours later, Henrik had just finished feeding the animals and was playing "fetch the stick" with Zeb. The pickup stopped next to the house; the doors opened and Henrik walked forward to greet the emerging passengers.

"Henrik, these are my parents, Becca and Ken Martin," Skye said.

"Pleased to meet you," Henrik said, shaking the hand of the trim, balding man with a pleasant smile. Then he turned to the dark haired woman with chocolate brown eyes and a contagious smile. "Pleased to meet you, Becca."

"Good to meet you, Henrik. We've heard so much about you," Becca enthused.

Henrik looked at Bo and Skye. "I hope it wasn't all bad."

"Not at all. They say you're a great guy," Becca said. Her smiling eyes shifted away from Henrik to something across the yard. "Oh my goodness, Skye, I must see your Belgians!" She was halfway to the fence by the time she finished speaking.

"As you can see, no grass grows under her feet," Ken remarked to Henrik. "My wife may be pushing 60, but when it comes to working with animals, she can out-do many people half her age."

"I believe it," Henrik agreed, watching the two women approach the horses. Becca didn't look a day over 40, he thought.

"Let's take the luggage inside and find some coffee," Bo said.

"Sounds good to me," replied Ken.

They ate lunch at Grandma's that day, and when Henrik saw

Becca and her mother side by side, he realized how much they resembled each other. Despite the fact that Grandma wore her hair pulled back under a covering while Becca's dark brown hair seemed to have a will of its own, and despite the contrast of Grandma's conservative Amish dress to Becca's boots and jeans, they were obviously mother and daughter. The same eyes extended a warm welcome to everyone, and the same dimple danced at the corner of their mouths.

After lunch Henrik and Kevin, who lived with his family in the same yard as Grandma, went outside to build a snowman. There was barely enough snow to accomplish their task, but an hour later, a small sturdy snowman the same size as Kevin stood in front of his house. Henrik took a picture of the happy little Amish boy standing next to his snowman. He respected the Amish belief of not having their pictures taken, but he knew they wouldn't mind if he kept the picture for himself.

Henrik spent most of the afternoon playing with Kevin and the rest of Caleb and Emma's kids. He walked with them to the old tree house in the pasture, pulled them in the little red wagon pretending to be a horse with "reins" around his neck, and joined in every game the children could dream up. They seldom had a tall strong teenager willing to do whatever they wanted, and they took full advantage of the opportunity. Henrik had never spent this much time with children, and he was surprised at how much fun he had.

Later in the afternoon, when it was time to go home, Skye said she wanted to walk, and invited Henrik to come with her. He started to protest, saying he'd had all the exercise he needed that afternoon, but when she said she wanted to talk to him, he agreed to the mile long trek home.

"I want to tell you the story of how my twin sister and I ended up with our adoptive parents," Skye said as they walked along the sand road. Typical of Kansas weather, today's warm sunshine had melted most of yesterday's snow.

"Okay," Henrik replied, and then listened as Skye recounted the strange circumstances surrounding the birth of her and Angela. She told him about the pregnant teenager that Ken picked up along the road near their home in Pennsylvania, the birth of the young woman's twin daughters just hours later, and then her sudden and mysterious departure soon after their birth.

"She left a note saying she wanted Ken and Becca to have her babies," Skye said. "Obviously, it was a very unusual way to become parents, but Mom and Dad believed it was God's plan, so they adopted us."

"Did you ever see your mother again?"

"Our biological mother? Yes—that's another long story. The short answer is that yes, I know her and we keep in touch—sort of. As far as my biological father, I have no idea who or where he is.

"Some people might say that us being adopted was partially responsible for my rebelliousness," Skye continued. "I don't know. I only know that Angela was the perfect daughter, and I wasn't. I was always pushing the edges, and Angela was always protecting me. Angela made a commitment to God as a teenager, but I said I had too much living to do to be stuck with religion."

Henrik could understand that.

"What I didn't realize was that I wasn't really living at all. As I got older, I abused my mind and body more and more. With my diabetes, I was actually killing myself. My parents tried to talk to me, but I wasn't into listening to them. After all, what do parents know?"

Henrik understood that too.

"It took Angela's death to bring me around to my senses. Up until then, I thought my life was mine to live as I chose. Now I've given it up to God. That's made all the difference in the world," Skye paused. "Surely you've seen that kind of thing in school—the difference between kids who are connected to God and those that aren't."

Of course he'd seen that. The goody-goody's versus the party lovers. That's the way he'd defined it.

"And it isn't that the Christian kids are boring and the non-Christian kids have more fun, if you think about it," Skye continued. "It's more like the Christian kids know what's important in life, and the others are looking all over to find it."

Henrik thought about that for a moment. "I think that's too general a statement," he said finally. "I know Christian kids who don't have it all together, and I know kids that don't go to church and they're good kids."

"You're right. Christians don't have it all together, and a lot of non-Christians are good people."

"So what's your point?"

"God made each of us with a hole in our heart that only God can fill. We can look a lot of other places for things to fill that hole, but nothing really works. And the neat thing is, when you put God in that hole and accept Jesus as your savior, you get a bonus called the Holy Spirit," Skye looked at Henrik. "And that's when the fun begins."

A hole filled with God? Holy Spirit? Fun? The crunch of Henrik's big Nike shoes and Skye's boots on the sand road was the only noise for a long time. Henrik's head was spinning. Strangely, it wasn't the talk about God reverberating through his mind. No, it was something else—something that had been bothering him for several weeks. Suddenly a mental picture of Mattie and Selena popped into his head. He could almost feel their presence beside him.

Then he knew. Skye was right. He'd seen it.

TWENTY

SOON AFTER HIS ARRIVAL in Kansas, during an orientation meeting, Henrik and the other students were told, "You won't believe how fast the time flies after Christmas." At the beginning of the school year, ten months seemed like an eternity. By November he had settled into a comfortable routine, and when December rolled around he could honestly say he was enjoying his year away from home. But the time definitely didn't seem to "fly."

Then Henrik woke up one morning and realized it had happened after all. Three months had slipped by without him noticing, and it was April 1. He'd been preoccupied with basketball, school, Mattie and the youth group, a ski trip, Bo and Skye and her family, Winston and Mitch, and a weekend trip for exchange students. His stomach knotted when he turned the calendar page to April. In just two months he would return to Sweden.

The knot tightened when he remembered his parents were coming to Kansas. It certainly hadn't been his idea. Skye had told his parents they were welcome to stay with them if they wanted to come to see Henrik graduate from Rolling Prairie High School, and the next thing he knew his parents said they'd love to.

No one had asked what he thought of the idea. He tried to suggest they wait a year and then the three of them could come back to visit. But they'd made up their mind. They wanted to see their son walk across the stage of an American high school, wearing a cap and gown, and receive his diploma.

Henrik had changed a lot during the past eight months, and he wasn't ready to merge his world in Sweden with the one in Kansas. He got along better with Bo and Skye than with his own parents. At home, he fought his parents' attempts to control his life. Here, he'd adapted to rules and standards that were beginning to feel right and fair. How was he supposed to act when they were all together in the same house? It would be too confusing. He didn't want his parents to come, but of course he couldn't say that.

Bo and Skye were enthusiastic about meeting his parents, as was Mattie. But then, Mattie got enthused about a lot of things. She loved meeting new people. Give her a free evening, and she'd find something fun to do. Give her an hour at the coffee shop or in a bookstore, and she'd fill your head with all kinds of deep thoughts.

They'd become best friends, and Henrik had adjusted himself to being satisfied with that level of a relationship. If he'd learned one thing during the past few months, it was that he would have to adapt to new situations if he wanted to be happy. Agreeing to be friends and no more had solved the question of their physical involvement. Hopefully, it would also make their parting less painful, but Henrik wasn't sure about that. He did not like the thought of saying good-bye to Mattie at all.

Henrik always received a phone call or visit from his area representative on the first of each month. This time Kory stopped by after supper and asked Henrik if he'd like to run into Wellsford for a Coke.

While they sat at the Deutschland Restaurant, drinking Cokes and eating huge pieces of homemade pie, Henrik told Kory his parents were coming for his graduation.

"Great! It'll be fun for them to see your world here in Kansas,"

Kory answered. "Are you excited about seeing your parents?"

"Not really."

Kory paused, his fork in the air, and looked at Henrik. "Not really? Why?"

Henrik hesitated, not sure how to explain his feelings. "I don't know. It's just so different. I don't want to deal with them in my life here."

"Don't you get along with your parents?"

"They're okay. But they're so different from Bo and Skye. And when they're all in the same house, it'll be confusing."

"You're right. It can be frustrating, especially if one set of parents becomes jealous of the other, or if they tell you different things. I remember one situation where one set of parents said the kid could do something and the others said she couldn't. That makes it hard on everybody. But Henrik," Kory paused again and studied the young man seated across the table from him. "If they want to come, that's a good thing. They will know what you're talking about when you tell them about your year here. And it'll be nice for them to meet Bo and Skye, and to thank them personally for everything they've done for you."

"I know," Henrik sighed. "But I'm not the same guy I was at home. You know what I mean?"

"I sure do," Kory chuckled. "You aren't the same guy that stepped off the plane. You've changed a lot. It'll be great for your parents to see that."

"Maybe, maybe not."

"What do you mean?"

Henrik took a bite of his peanut butter pie and savored it while he contemplated his answer. Finally he said, "It's hard to explain."

"Let me try," Kory said. In Sweden you were used to doing what you wanted to, and you fought with your parents when you didn't get your way. You were even a bit arrogant, perhaps?

"Just a guess, Henrik, just a guess," Kory grinned. "I'm also guessing maybe you didn't want to be an exchange student, but your parents insisted. Now, the last thing you want to admit is that they were right and this year has been good for you. Am I right?"

It was Henrik's turn to study Kory. "How did you come up with that?"

"I've been an area rep long enough. I've seen it before. It was just a hunch, from what I saw of your attitude and behavior in the beginning."

"I guess you're right."

"So what you need to figure out now is how to be okay about your parents seeing the change in you. They'll like it, Henrik. It's something to be proud of. You'll just have to swallow a little bit of pride in the process."

"Yeah."

"I'd like for you to do me a favor. Sometime between now and the first of May, I'd like for you to write down what's happened to you this year. I think it will help you see the processes you went through, and to feel good about your parents seeing who you are now. I would also like a copy to put in the orientation packets for next year's students. Something they can read from someone who's been in their shoes. Would you be willing to do that?"

"Ah, I'm not much of a writer."

"You don't have to be. Just think it through and put it down on paper."

Henrik grinned. "Okay, maybe. But it'll cost you more than a piece of pie. I think we're talking a steak dinner.

Kory laughed. "You've got a deal."

Prom was one of those American high school traditions that exchange students were always curious about, and Henrik had two girls who were eager to take him to Rolling Prairie's prom the third Saturday in April.

Selena continued to show a strong interest in Henrik, even though he hadn't asked her out since the party at her house. Now she had invited him to the prom, promising him a great time, including a limousine ride and an all-night party afterwards. What guy in his right mind would refuse an invitation like that?

Mattie said she'd also love to take him. Henrik weighed the choice between a hot date and a nice friendly evening. A voice in his head said a guy only gets to go to prom once, so go for the good time. That voice had the cheering support of Winston and Mitch, who couldn't understand why Henrik had never dated Selena. On the other hand, why should he go with somebody he didn't care about, and risk damaging his friendship with Mattie? He knew what Bo and Skye would say if he told them about his dilemma.

Selena cornered him at his locker after school a week before prom. "I've got the limo rented," she gushed. "It'll be so cool!"

"I haven't said I'd go with you."

"You mean somebody else asked you and you said yes?"

"No. I'm just saying you're assuming I'll go with you because you already rented a limo."

"Well I couldn't wait forever. I wanted to make sure we could get one."

"So the limo takes us to the prom, and then what?"

"It picks us up afterwards and we cruise Wellsford, then we head for Vicksburg."

"What happens there?"

"We cruise and end up at a motel. A bunch of us have four rooms rented, and there's a pool and stuff. We stay up all night, then go home and crash."

"The limo takes us home too?"

"No, silly. There'll be kids there with cars and we can catch a ride back with them."

It did sound like fun, Henrik thought. "I'll let you know tomorrow."

At that moment Mattie walked up and asked if Henrik was ready to go home. She smiled at Selena, who smirked in return.

"See you tomorrow, Swede. I'll be waiting for your answer," Selena's tantalizing words hung in the air.

Henrik found other things to talk to Mattie about during most of the drive home, but he knew they had to discuss the prom issue. He owed it to both Selena and Mattie to make a decision.

"About prom. . ." He finally broached the subject.

"I know. You have to decide who you're going with," Mattie responded. "I have to tell you, I can't offer a limo or a party in a motel all night."

"How did you know that's what Selena and her group are doing?"

"The whole school knows, Henrik."

"What can you offer?" Henrik teased.

"Just plain ol' me and my car. After the dance, a bunch of us will probably go to somebody's house and then go out for breakfast early in the morning."

"Whose house? What will you do there?"

"A couple of us had an idea about a flashlight game during the night, out in some trees. But we haven't found the right place yet."

"What do you mean, a flashlight game?"

"Kind of like a huge hide and seek. I've heard of kids who do it. They wear dark clothes and it's a lot of fun."

Henrik knew that Bo and Skye's place would be perfect for that kind of game, but if he suggested it to Mattie, he would be committed to going with her. He laughed at his options. He could ride in a limousine with one of the sexiest women in the school, and go to an all-night party in a motel. Or he could ride with Mattie in her car and play hide and seek with her friends in the trees.

What a choice.

TWENTY-ONE

HE TOLD HIMSELF he had a right to go to the prom with whomever he wanted; that it didn't matter if Bo and Skye were disappointed with his choice; that he deserved a true prom experience after adhering to their rules for so long. He told himself that being with Selena and her friends did not mean he had to drink with them; that no matter how tempted he might be, he would not jeopardize his last two months in the States.

Selena was right—the limo was cool. When Henrik slid into the back seat of the long white car, he was surprised by how much room there was inside. He was also surprised to discover that Selena had already started drinking. He smelled the liquor on her breath when she leaned against him and pinned a rose to the lapel of his tuxedo. She looked incredibly stunning in a long, tight black dress that enhanced every curve of her perfect figure, and was slit up the side to reveal her shapely legs. There was no doubt that Selena was the sexiest girl at Rolling Prairie High School.

"What do you think?" she asked, still fiddling with the flower on his lapel.

"I love it! I can't believe how big it is in here!"

"Big enough to move around and do whatever we want," Selena smiled, stroking the leather seat beside her. "There's even a TV and a bar in the corner."

Henrik turned on the TV and opened the small refrigerator.

It was empty.

"Don't worry about that. We've got our own stuff." Henrik glanced at Selena's long legs as she slide across the seat and reached for her purse on the floor. "Between this and what the other kids are bringing, we're set."

Henrik grinned. He didn't plan to risk drinking—getting caught could put him in big trouble. On the other hand, exchange students weren't sent home for enjoying themselves, and it had been a long time since he'd been with a girl.

The junior class at Rolling Prairie High School had decorated the school cafeteria for the prom's catered banquet, and Henrik was surprised at how nice the cafeteria looked. The juniors had out-done themselves. He escorted Selena to their table, but they were barely seated when she excused herself. "Gotta run to the ladies room," she said to Henrik, then turned to the girl across the table from them. "Mari, would you like to come with me?"

Henrik watched them leave. "Girls are so strange about going to the bathroom together," he commented to Mitch, who was Mari's date.

"Yeah, but this time I wouldn't mind going along," Mitch responded quietly. "Either that, or else I'd like to borrow Selena's purse for a few minutes."

Henrik grinned back at Mitch, but he felt a twinge inside. Drinking at a party later was one thing, but why did Selena have to start this early?

After what seemed like a long time, the two girls returned. They were both giggling. The two couples made small talk during the banquet and when they finished eating, the girls excused themselves again. When they returned, Selena leaned close to Henrik. The smell of alcohol and strong perfume reminded him of parties he'd attended in Sweden.

"Do you want something to help you relax before the

dance?" she whispered in his ear.

He'd been wondering how long it would take for her to offer him a drink. He looked around. The senior class chaperone was staring at their table.

"Maybe later," he whispered back.

They left the table and moved with the other students to the commons area for the dance. Again, Henrik was impressed with the decorations. Shimmering streamers, soft lights and a spinning lighted globe transformed the area into an attractive dance floor. A disc jockey from a Vicksburg radio station sat in a corner on a raised platform and spun the CDs. Not bad for a high school in the middle of the Kansas prairie, Henrik conceded.

Two dances into the evening, Selena asked Henrik if he wanted to go outside with her. He knew what "outside" meant, and declined. He wasn't going to risk being caught drinking while they were still at the school. Selena seemed angry when he refused her offer, and she disappeared with Winston, Mitch, and Mari. Left alone, Henrik looked for Mattie and finally spotted her with a group of girls at the side of the room. He walked over to talk to them.

"How was the limo ride?" Mattie asked.

"Pretty nice. There's a lot of room inside those things!"

"We girls thought about getting one together, but it seemed like a lot of money for the short time we'd use it. Besides, it's more fun if you have a date," Mattie said, and Henrik noticed a trace of bitterness in her voice. "Isn't that right?"

What could he say?

"Yeah, I guess it is," he answered lamely.

"Oh, there you are!" Selena slipped into the group and took Henrik's arm. "I've been looking for you. Hope it's okay if I take him away, girls," she threw a sardonic half-smile in their direction and then led Henrik toward the dance floor.

"Let's dance, Swede-man!"

They danced every song during the next half-hour. Henrik's eyes feasted on Selena's body in her form-fitting dress, and when the DJ played a slow dance, he held her close. Afterward, Selena held onto him for a moment and whispered in his ear, "I need some fresh air. Take me outside. Please."

This time he agreed, although he wasn't sure why. He led Selena through the darkened commons area to the front door and when they stepped outside, he heard some guys talking in the parking lot.

"Come Swede-man," Selena giggled. She led him toward a small group of prom-goers standing next to a car. They were passing a bottle around. Selena took a swig and handed the bottle to Henrik. He took a swallow, and felt the whiskey burn its way down his throat and leave a warm spot in his stomach.

The others had obviously been drinking for some time. Henrik was the only one among them who wasn't affected by the alcohol, but he knew if he kept drinking, he'd soon be in the same shape they were. He passed on the next round. Common sense dictated that drinking on school property was a bad idea, but these kids didn't seem to care.

The group headed back to the dance, and for the next hour, Henrik enjoyed himself. Then Selena said she wanted to go outside again, but this time Henrik said no. "Go ahead," he told her. "I'll be in here."

"Oh Swede, please."

To avoid making a scene, he wandered around the darkened room with Selena, looking for Winston and some of the others who'd been outside earlier. They found Winston with a group of his buddies in one of the corners, and Selena immediately latched onto him.

"Hey Swede, we're gonna slip out for a bit—come along!" Winston offered.

"Not right now," Henrik answered. "I'll wait for you inside."

He felt foolish hanging around by himself, and looked again for Mattie. Soon he was dancing with her and her friends, and when the DJ played a popular country song, he let them teach him a line dance. He almost forgot about Selena, and when one of girls made a comment about his "disappearing date," he laughed and shrugged it off. But he wondered what had happened to her and the rest of the group.

After several more dances, when they still hadn't returned, he walked toward the front entrance of the school. One of the chaperones was standing by the door. Outside, Henrik could see Selena and her group approaching the building. She opened the door and walked through. "Just a minute, Selena," the chaperone said. "The rest of you hold it right there."

Selena stared at Henrik, her look of surprise reflected on the faces of the other students. "We just went out for some fresh air. It was getting hot in there," Selena explained to the chaperone.

"Right. You've also been drinking. We heard this might be going on. I have strict orders not to allow anyone inside who's been drinking."

Selena and her friends looked at each other, then stared at the chaperone. "You can't keep us out of our own prom!" she challenged.

"If you've been drinking, I certainly can."

"Screw it!" one of the guys exclaimed. "We don't need this stupid prom anyway. Let's get outta here." He turned and stormed out the door.

"Henrik!" Selena called.

The chaperon looked at Henrik, then back at Selena.

"He's my date!" Selena whined. "You're banning me from my date?"

"Henrik, do you want to leave with them?" the chaperon asked. Henrik wavered. The limo, the all-night party in a motel with the hottest girl in high school, the kind of prom to tell the guys at home about——he'd really wanted that experience.

"No thanks," he answered the chaperon, staring past him at Selena. He turned and walked back to the dance.

He felt like such a jerk, crawling back to Mattie and telling her what had happened. He knew she was disappointed with his choice to go with Selena. And now he was begging her for a ride home after the dance.

But when he asked, the sweet smiling Mattie was back. Sure, he could hang out with the girls if he wanted to, she said.

They left when the dance ended at midnight. Henrik rode in Mattie's car, along with three of her girlfriends. Another carload of girls followed them as they cruised Wellsford's Main Street a few times. They laughed a lot, stopped for two Mennonite car dances, and by 12:30 they were headed for one of the girl's homes.

"You can just take me home if you want," Henrik told Mattie. "I don't want to get in the way of what you girls have planned. I feel kinda stupid being the only guy here."

"Doesn't bother me if it doesn't bother them, but we can stop and take a vote," Mattie said lightly, slowing the car and pulling to the side of the road. The other car slowed and pulled in behind her.

"Not another car dance!" one of the girls hollered as they spilled out of the second car.

"Nope, this is a vote!" Mattie answered. "Please line up and be prepared to cast your ballot." Laughing, the girls lined up against the vehicles.

"The question before us is whether or not to allow one Henrik Svensson, also known as Swede, to spend the night with us," Mattie announced. "Is there any discussion before we take the vote?"

Henrik stood apart from them and looked at the seven girls in prom dresses, standing in a row along a Kansas country road in the middle of the night, the darkness illuminated by the car's headlights. It could be a sobriety test, except there was no cop or patrol car with flashing lights, and no trace of alcohol. These girls are drunk on fun, he thought. It wasn't the first time he'd noticed that with Mattie and her friends.

"Hearing no discussion, I call for the vote," Mattie announced. "Swede, if you don't mind sticking your fingers in your ears and closing your eyes, we can have a confidential vote."

Henrik obeyed. If the guys in Sweden could see him now...

They seemed to take a long time to decide. Suddenly a car horn blew loudly. Henrik jumped, opened his eyes and realized he was the only one still standing on the road.

"You're in," Mattie giggled. "Would you like to join us in the car?"

TWENTY-TWO

BY MONDAY MORNING the entire school knew what had happened at the prom. Most of the gossip centered on Selena and her friends being kicked out for drinking. Henrik's decision to remain at the dance rather than leave with Selena brought mixed reactions. Selena snubbed him. Winston and Mitch let Swede know what a great party he missed at the motel. Mattie's friends were thrilled that Henrik had chosen to spend the night playing games and eating breakfast with them. Mattie, in her usual sweet, easy-going manner, ignored the gossip and all the speculation that followed.

Henrik knew he'd made a statement that night. Watching the kids drinking in the parking lot, he'd begun to realize how foolish they were. Teenagers who thought a good time could only be found in a bottle of illegal booze were not cool. They said and did stupid things that weren't the least bit funny if you were sober.

In sharp contrast was the good time he'd had with Mattie and her friends. The silly roadside vote was only the beginning. They'd played flashlight hide and seek in a pasture where the creepy hooting of screech owls and the eerie howling of coyotes added a touch of drama to the adventure. The girls screamed a lot. Henrik didn't scream but his heart skipped a beat or two when his flashlight beam caught a shiny black and white skunk crossing in front of him, and when a hawk swept down from a nearby tree.

Later, they'd built a bonfire and told scary stories, then decided to fly a kite. Henrik couldn't see the point of flying a kite in the dark of night but he had gotten used to the girls' strange ideas. Not having a point was often the point itself.

By the time they drove into Vicksburg for breakfast at an all-night restaurant shortly before dawn, Henrik's stomach hurt from laughing and he had learned a new definition of a "good time."

Monday evening, Henrik sat at his desk and tried to concentrate on his homework. His eyes fell on a note he'd stuck to his calendar. "Kory paper." Kory wanted him to write some reflections about his year in Kansas. He knew Kory would get a kick out of what had happened at the prom. What the heck—he wasn't getting his homework done anyway. He opened a new screen on his computer and typed, "MY YEAR IN THE UNITED STATES."

Prom was the first of three traditional events for seniors at Rolling Prairie High School. The second was a senior trip. This year the class had voted to go to Kansas City. Their itinerary called for a visit to the Arabia Steamboat Museum, a shopping excursion, a dinner dance on a ferry, and a night in a hotel on the Plaza. Henrik had no idea what to expect, but he was looking forward to the weekend away from home.

The 80 members of the senior class clambered aboard two school buses early on the morning of the first Saturday in May. Mattie asked Henrik to sit with her, and he couldn't think of another person with whom he'd rather spend two hours on a bumpy bus.

They talked easily about a variety of things, then 30 minutes into the trip, after a pause in their conversation, Mattie said, "Henrik."

"Yes?"

"I was mad at you when you went to the prom with Selena."

"I know."

"I feel bad about it now, but I'd really been hoping to go with you. Prom is a big deal here in America, and it's my senior year and all."

"I'm sorry, Mattie. If I'd known how it would turn out..."

"That's the problem, Henrik. You can't make decisions that way, because you never know how things will turn out. You don't know! You have to make good decisions at the time so the chances are good that it will turn out right. Don't you see?"

Henrik nodded.

"We all make bad choices at times, but you have to go with the choice that has the best odds. You've gotta admit, the odds weren't exactly stacked in your favor, being out with Selena and her friends."

"I know, I know, I know," Henrik answered. "I get the message."

"Sorry."

A long silence followed, and Henrik was beginning to wish he had a reason to go sit with someone else for a while.

"When do you go home?" Mattie asked.

"Now you're trying to get rid of me?"

"You know better than that, Henrik," Mattie replied.

"Yeah, I do. I think it's June 2."

"A month. I can't believe it."

"Me neither."

"I remember the first time I saw you—-the morning you walked into church with Bo and Skye."

"I remember you, too. You were about the only thing worthwhile in church that morning."

"Henrik!"

"You know what I mean! I wasn't used to that church thing."

"I know. And in a month, you won't have to worry about going any more."

"That's right."

"What's the first thing you'll do when you get home? Throw a party and get wasted?" Mattie asked in a matter-of-fact voice, without condemnation or celebration.

"If you'd asked me that a few months ago, I'd have said 'For sure!' But now. . ."

"Now what?"

"Now I'll probably take my friends out for a smashing game of flashlight hide and seek."

Mattie hit Henrik playfully on the shoulder. "Now you are making fun of me, Henrik Svensson!"

"Oh no, not me. Never! In fact, I was thinking of asking you to come to Sweden to show my friends how to play flashlight-in-a-pasture and fly-a-kite-in-the-dark."

"No you weren't."

"Yes I was. I'm serious. You should come visit me. Sweden is a beautiful country. I'd love to show you around."

"I'd love to come, Henrik," Mattie's dark eyes danced with anticipation. "I just don't know how I'd ever save enough money to do that."

They were silent for a few minutes, then Mattie spoke quietly. "It would be easier to say good-bye if I knew it wasn't forever."

Forever. For the first time, the reality of his leaving hit Henrik hard. His life in Kansas that now felt so comfortable was nearly over. Forever. He'd be getting on a plane and saying good-bye to Mattie, Bo, Skye, Winston, Mitch and Grandma Bontrager. He'd be leaving one world for another. Rolling Prairie High School, the farm, the Kansas sunsets, the dumb Mennonite car dances with the girls—in just one month they would only be memories.

"Are you going to try out for the commencement speech?"

Thankfully, Mattie changed the subject.

"What do you mean?"

"There are always two seniors who talk at graduation. One is the valedictorian, and the class selects the other one. Kids who want to give the speech have to present it to the class ahead of time, and then the class votes."

"Why would anybody want to do that?"

"It's a chance to thank the teachers and reflect on your school years. Obviously it's not something everybody would want to do, but sometimes there are surprises. Last year the class clown did it, and it was hilarious."

"Are you going to try out?"

"I think so. I've had a great high school experience, and I'd enjoy reflecting on it."

"You'll get it. I can't think of anybody else who could do it better."

"We'll see."

Henrik and Mattie spent most of the weekend together. They were both amazed at the Arabia Steamboat Museum where artifacts, preserved in the mud since the boat sank in the Missouri River in the late 1800's, were displayed. They shopped together, dined and danced together, and when it was time to go to their separate rooms for the night, they hugged each other for a long time. Henrik wanted a kiss too, but settled for a tender brush of his lips on Mattie's forehead. He knew not to push the limits. Their friendship was too valuable.

Everyone slept in on Sunday morning, then after a huge breakfast and a walk around the Plaza, the group boarded the bus for the trip back home. They unloaded at the high school, and Mattie drove Henrik to his house. She stayed awhile, and was still there when Kory drove into the yard.

"Hey, Henrik," Kory said, stepping out of the car and walking to the deck where Henrik and Mattie were enjoying the spring evening air. "How's it going?"

"Fine, Kory. This is Mattie, a friend from school. Mattie—Kory."

Mattie and Kory exchanged greetings, and Kory sat down next to them. They talked about the weekend, about how fast the year had gone and how it would feel to go back to Sweden.

"Did you get my paper written?" Kory asked. "You know, the one where you tell future exchange students what you learned this year about how to succeed in an American high school?"

"Yeah, I wrote something. It's nothing special, but you can have it." Henrik got up and went to his room to get the paper. He returned in a moment and handed it to Kory. "You can trash it if you want," he said.

"May I read that?" Mattie asked. "Please?"

"Ah, I don't know," Henrik frowned.

"After all I've done for you?" Mattie pouted. "All the miles I've driven hauling you around? Surely they're worth something."

"They're worth a lot, but I don't think the paper is."

"Let me be the judge of that, okay?"

"Oh, whatever," he conceded with a sigh.

Kory handed the paper to Mattie, then he and Henrik talked while Mattie read. Henrik couldn't concentrate on what Kory was saying—he was busy trying to recall what he'd written, and wishing Mattie wasn't reading it.

She was silent when she finished. Misty-eyed, she finally looked up and said quietly, "That is powerful, Henrik."

He shifted uneasily in his chair. Whatever he'd written, Henrik certainly hadn't thought it would make a person cry.

"You've got me curious now," Kory said, reaching for the paper.

"You have to promise me one thing," Mattie said to Henrik.

"You have to promise me you'll read this to the class when we vote on our commencement speaker."

"No way," Henrik's answer was instantaneous.

"I'm serious, Henrik."

"And I am too."

"If you don't, I will."

"What? You'll read my paper?"

"You better believe it. I'll say it's yours, but you're too chicken to present it."

"You don't have a copy of it, and Kory's not giving it to you," Henrik looked threateningly at his area rep.

"Kory?" Mattie pleaded.

"Gosh, it's his paper, Mattie. I can't just hand it over without his permission."

"That's right," Henrik leaned back in his chair and relaxed.

"At the same time," Kory continued, "If it's as good as Mattie says it is, I would sure encourage you to listen to her. What's this about reading it to the class?"

"We choose one of our commencement speakers from seniors who try out for the honor," Mattie explained. "I think Henrik should give this speech."

"I'll die before I give a speech at commencement," Henrik stated. "So just give it up, okay?"

TWENTY-THREE

"IF YOU HAD TOLD ME ten months ago that I'd be giving a commencement speech, I'd have called you insane." Henrik's eyes swept across the crowded auditorium. His heart was pounding and his hands gripping the side of the podium were sweating. "If you'd told me two weeks ago, I would still have said you were crazy. But here I am." He paused and took a deep breath. "Here I am."

He glanced down at the paper in front of him and began reading it aloud. "You should know that I didn't want to come to the U.S. as an exchange student. I came because my parents kind of insisted on it. My sisters and brother were exchange students and they all had great experiences, but I didn't like having to do things just because they did. It seemed to me that I was always expected to follow their example."

Henrik's parents were in the audience. He couldn't look at them. He kept reading.

"When I agreed to go, I hoped I'd be sent to California where the good-looking babes are." A snicker spread through the auditorium. Henrik smiled and relaxed a bit. "You can't imagine how disappointed I was when I heard I was going to Kansas. My friends in Sweden teased me about what I'd find here—just cowboys, cows, flat land and people who go to church a lot." Another chuckle rippled through the crowd. "When I got here, it was ungodly hot and flat. And yes, I had to go to church right away. I wasn't thrilled about being here, and I'm sure you all noticed. In fact, to be honest, I acted like a jerk. I'm sure you noticed that too."

Henrik looked up from his paper and his eyes found Mattie sitting in the row of graduates. She smiled up at him.

"Back home in Sweden, I thought I had friends," Henrik continued. "I thought I was good with the girls. I thought I could conquer anyone, anything, any situation. My idea of conquering Kansas was to get away with as much as I could, find a girlfriend (or two or three), and have a good time despite the rules and regulations of the organization. I guess I was pretty arrogant."

Henrik glanced at the audience. Every eye was on him. They can't believe what they're hearing, he thought. And I can't believe I'm saying this.

"To be honest, I don't know why anybody put up with me, but you did. And because you did, I got used to your way of life, and I learned some things.

"One important thing I learned in church that first Sunday morning was that Kansas actually has good-looking girls, too!"

The audience laughed again, and when Henrik caught Mattie's eye, she covered her face with her hands in mock embarrassment.

"I learned very early that another word for a 'woman screaming in the night' is 'peacock.' I got used to the peacocks and other animals on Bo and Skye's farm, and I hope they got used to me, too.

"I learned that if you're going to play football at Rolling Prairie High School, you have to get up way too early in the morning. But I found out that early practices are almost worth the pain when we win the game.

"I learned about Mennonite car dances and flashlight hide-and-seek. Thanks to a group of crazy girls, I found out how to have fun without breaking any organization rules or Kansas laws.

"I learned more about American history and government

than I ever wanted to know, and I would like to invite Mr. Estee to Sweden to study my country's history and government in the Swedish language. Then, Mr. Estee, I would be happy to devise a test for you, too."

The audience, especially the students, appreciated that comment. Henrik realized his hands were no longer gripping the sides of the podium.

"I learned that the Amish are real people underneath those conservative clothes. Thanks to my host mom, Skye, my family now includes Amish people. I got to know and love Skye's grandfather—we called him Dawdi—and when he died, I felt a big loss. There was so much I could still learn from him, and suddenly he was gone.

"I've had to do some things I wouldn't normally do. I've had to sit back and accept things that were different, and I've learned to listen more and talk less.

"I've discovered that a walk under the Kansas full moon with someone who means a lot to me is a greater treasure than anything money could buy. I've learned that gazing into the eyes of a beautiful girl and kissing her softly left a more powerful impact on my soul than 'conquering' a girl ever could.

"I've learned that the people we hang out with affect who we are and who we become."

Henrik flipped to the next page of his paper. He was almost done. He looked at the audience in front of him. There, in the second row behind the graduates, were Bo, Skye, his parents, and Grandma Bontrager. *People affect who we are and who we become.* His own words echoed in his mind.

"And now I want to say a few words to some very special people," he heard himself saying. His heart raced. He didn't have this on paper. There were no notes to follow.

"First, to my parents," Henrik gulped, finding his parents in the audience. "This is hard to say, Mom and Dad, but thank you for sending me here. I'm not the same person that you put on that plane. I left Sweden thinking I knew it all, but I learned a lot here. I guess I didn't know everything after all."

Henrik saw Skye reach over and clasp his mother's hand. His mom's face was crinkled in a half-smile, half-crying sort of way. His father looked proud. Henrik couldn't remember his father ever looking at him with that expression on his face before.

"Bo and Skye—what can I say," Henrik continued. "You loved and accepted me when I didn't deserve it. You taught me to be trustworthy by trusting me when I didn't deserve it. You treated me like your own son. I will never forget you." Skye wiped her eyes, and Bo put his arm around her shoulders.

"Grandma Bontrager, thank you for accepting me. You and Dawdi made me feel like a part of your family, even though our lifestyles are so different. I never felt your disapproval for anything I said or did. I just felt your love all the time. Thank you."

Henrik took a deep breath. He couldn't stop there. He had to mention some of his classmates.

"Winston and Mitch, thanks for being my friends. It would have been a long year without you guys to talk to."

"Mattie." Quiet laughter rippled among the students. Someone let out a wolf whistle and Henrik felt a flush creeping across his face.

"I learned a lot about relationships from you, Mattie," he rushed ahead. "Thank you for caring about this guy named Swede."

Somebody let out a long "AHHH HH HHH," and the audience laughed. Henrik grinned, then looked at Winston. "I wasn't going to say this, Winston, but you asked for it. At least Mattie didn't get me into trouble and almost sent home."

Winston gave him a thumbs up—he didn't care—and Henrik laughed.

"There are many more people I could thank," Henrik continued, "But I need to wrap this up. It's time to get on with what you all came for—to see us walk across this stage and get our diplomas.

"Today we will graduate and leave the halls of Rolling Prairie High School behind us," he continued reading his last page of notes. "We are not only leaving the school; we are leaving friends behind as well. My friends, this is my top ten list of what I have learned and how I want to change as a result of my time in Kansas. Maybe there's something here for you, too, as you take the next steps in your lives:

"I want to listen more and talk less.

"I want to turn off the electronic world often enough to discover myself, my friends, and the outside world around me. I want to walk under the full moon more often.

"I want to remember that looking into a girl's soul is more important than checking out her body.

"I want friends for life, not objects for the moment.

"I want to know people whose culture may be different but whose hearts are good and true.

"I want to believe in a person until he or she gives me reason not to, and then I want to give them a second chance.

"I want to have friends of all ages.

"I want to have fun without the influence of alcohol.

"I want to work on my relationship with God.

"I want to give myself to someone the way you have given yourselves to me. I may never see any of you again, but I promise I will never forget you and my family here in Kansas. You took a jerk and helped him become a man."

TWENTY-FOUR

THAT EVENING, Bo and Skye hosted a graduation party for Henrik at their home. His parents were there, and Mattie, Grandma Bontrager and Emma and Caleb with all of their kids. Kory and a few people from the church stopped by, and Winston and Mitch had promised to come later, when their own parties were over.

"Great speech, Henrik," Kory said as they sat on the deck, eating fancy little sandwiches and other party refreshments.

"Thanks."

"What I'm dying to know is, how did she get you to do it?" Kory grinned at Mattie, seated next to Henrik.

"She blackmailed me."

"I did not!" Mattie exclaimed. "I simply said if he wouldn't do it, I wouldn't come visit him. And I got the class sponsor to read it and put the pressure on."

"Blackmail and high pressure," Kory nodded. "Good job, Mattie. Now Henrik, aren't you glad you did it?"

"I guess—now that it's over."

Henrik's little Amish buddy, Kevin, sidled up to him and whispered, "When are you going to open your presents?"

"I don't know. Do you want to help me?"

Kevin nodded shyly.

"Did you bring me a present?" Henrik teased.

Kevin grinned. "Yep," he said.

"Well where is it?"

"In the buggy."

"How can I open it if it's still in the buggy?"

"They have to stay there until you open your presents."

"'They?' What do you have in your buggy, anyway?"

"It's a surprise!" The little boy's eyes shone with excitement.

"Well then, you'd better help me finish these sandwiches on my plate so we can start opening the presents!" Henrik said.

A pile of gifts had been accumulating on a table at the corner of the deck. The guests gathered around to watch Henrik open them.

"Kevin says he left my present in their buggy, so maybe we should start with that. Do you want to bring it here or shall I go with you to the buggy?"

"You come along." Kevin took Henrik's hand and led him across the yard. When they reached the buggy, Kevin pointed to a box on the floor. "Can you lift this down?" he asked.

"Sure." Henrik pulled the box out of the buggy and felt it move. "What's in here?" he asked, pretending to be frightened. "A snake? Something that will bite me?"

"No," Kevin giggled. "Look inside!"

"Let's take it up to the deck and show everybody."

When Henrik opened the box a few moments later, two fluffy, blue-eyed, yellow kittens stared up at him and meowed.

"Oh my goodness! Kittens!" Henrik exclaimed. "You gave me kittens!"

"Kevin insisted," Emma explained. "I told him you probably couldn't take them home with you, but he didn't care. He wanted you to have those kittens. I asked Skye, and she said it's okay if they stay here when you go home."

Henrik laughed, taking one of the kittens out of the box. "I suppose I could try putting them in my suitcase."

"Could you do that?" Kevin asked, his eyes big with hope.

"No, probably not. But I'll enjoy them until I go home, and then I'll leave them here with Bo and Skye, if that's okay with you."

"Okay," Kevin agreed.

The next present was from Mattie. He opened it and found a small shiny silver flashlight. Engraved on the side were the words, "You light up my life. Love, Mattie."

"Wow, Mattie, I love it!"

"I didn't want you to be without a flashlight when you go back and teach your friends how to play flashlight hide-and-seek."

Henrik chuckled, but his heart ached. He wouldn't be teaching anyone the game. He was going home to a different world, one he was no longer used to.

He opened the present from Bo and Skye next. Inside was an album full of pictures to remind him of his year in Kansas.

"Oh, man, thanks! You knew I wasn't doing this for myself, so you did it for me!" Henrik exclaimed.

"Skye said you've got to have a photo album so you'll remember us," Bo said.

"I'll remember you guys, don't worry. But this is so cool!"

The last gift was from Grandma Bontrager. The present was large and cumbersome, and Henrik set it on the floor of the deck. When he tore off the wrapping paper and saw what it was, he immediately lifted it back onto the table.

"Let me help you open it," Skye said, coming to his side. "You take one corner and I'll take another."

What they unfolded was a hand-sewn Amish quilt, but Henrik knew immediately it was much more than that. He recognized the fabric in some of the quilt pieces, taken from clothes he'd worn as a child! Those pieces were artistically arranged with traditional Amish fabrics into a beautiful pattern. He couldn't believe his eyes.

"How in the—?" Henrik wondered.

"Grandma Bontrager had the idea, and your mom sent her the pieces of material from your old clothes," Skye explained. "Grandma took it from there."

"I don't know if boys like quilts, but I figured you need something on your bed just like girls do," Grandma said.

"It's beautiful, Grandma, absolutely beautiful," Henrik said, standing up and taking the few steps to where Grandma was seated. He bent down and wrapped his long arms around the little Amish woman. "Thank you so much."

"You're welcome, Henrik."

"There's one more present," Kevin told Henrik when he returned to his seat. Henrik saw a small flat package that had been underneath the quilt. He picked it up and opened it slowly. Inside was a faded red bandanna, ironed and neatly folded. He took it out of the box and looked at Grandma.

"I wanted you to have one," she said softly. "Dawdi told me the night he died how much he liked you. He said you were figuring out who you are. He said he prays you'll find the way that is right and good. Take it as a memory of him."

The huge lump in Henrik's throat made talking difficult. And even if he could, what could he possibly say?

THIS CONCLUDES THE SKYE SERIES

OTHER BOOKS FROM
WILLOWSPRING DOWNS

JONAS SERIES

The Jonas Series was the brainchild of Maynard Knepp, a popular speaker on the Amish culture who grew up in an Amish family in central Kansas. Knepp and his wife Carol Duerksen, a freelance writer, collaborated to produce their first book, *Runaway Buggy*, released in October, 1995. The resounding success of that book encouraged them to continue, and the series grew to four books within 18 months. The books portray the Amish as real people who face many of the same decisions, joys and sorrows as everyone else, as well as those that are unique to their culture and tradition. Written in an easy-to-read style that appeals to a wide range of ages and diverse reader base — from elementary age children to folks in their 90s, from dairy farmers to PhDs — fans of the Jonas Series are calling it captivating, intriguing, can't-put-it-down reading.

RUNAWAY BUGGY

This book sweeps the reader into the world of an Amish youth trying to find his way "home." Not only does *Runaway Buggy* pull back a curtain to more clearly see a group of people, but it intimately reveals the heart of one of their sons struggling to become a young man all his own.

HITCHED

With *Hitched*, the second installment in the Jonas Series, the reader struggles with Jonas as he searches for the meaning of Christianity and tradition, and feels his bewilderment as he recognizes that just as there are Christians who are not Amish, there are Amish who are not Christians.

PREACHER

Book Three in the Jonas Series finds Jonas Bontrager the owner of a racehorse named Preacher, and facing dilemmas that only his faith can explain, and only his faith can help him endure.

BECCA

The fourth book in the Jonas Series invites readers to see the world through the eyes of Jonas Bontrager's 16-year-old daughter Becca, as she asks the same questions her father did, but in her own fresh and surprising ways.

SKYE SERIES

A spin-off of the much-loved Jonas Series, the Skye Series follows Jonas Bontrager's daughter Becca as she marries and becomes the mother of twin daughters, Angela and Skye. While Angela rests on an inner security of who she is and what life is about, Skye's journey takes her to very different places and situations. Through it all, she holds tightly to one small red piece of security—a bandanna her Amish grandfather gave her as a child.

TWINS

In the first book of the Skye Series, Becca and her husband Ken become the parents of twin daughters through very unusual circumstances—circumstances that weave the twins' lives together even as they are pulled apart by their separate destinies.

AFFAIR OF THE HEART

Not long after rock star Skye Martin settles into the Wellsford Amish community, the tongues begin to wag. She's been seen a lot lately with Ezra Yoder, an Amish man who always did seem to have secrets of his own.

Slickfester Dude
Tells Bedtime Stories
Life Lessons from our Animal Friends

by Carol Duerksen (& Slickfester Dude)

WillowSpring Downs is not only a publishing company — it's also a 120-acre piece of paradise in central Kansas that's home to a wide assortment of animals. Slickfester Dude, a black cat with three legs that work and one that doesn't, is one of those special animals. In a unique book that only a very observant cat could write, Slickfester Dude tells Carol a bedtime story every night — a story of life among the animals and what it can mean for everyone's daily life. This book will delight people from elementary age and up because the short stories are told in words that both children and adults can understand and take to heart. Along with strong, sensitive black and white story illustrations, the book includes Slickfester Dude's Photo Album of his people and animal friends at WillowSpring Downs.

VISIT OUR WEB SITES:

http://www.geocities.com/Eureka/Plaza/1638
http://www.geocities.com/Heartland/Ranch/7719

ORDER FORM

All titles are $9.95 each.

Jonas Series:

_____ copy/copies of *Runaway Buggy*

_____ copy/copies of *Hitched*

_____ copy/copies of *Preacher*

_____ copy/copies of *Becca*

_____ Jonas Series—all 4 books, $36.50

Skye Series:

_____ copy/copies of *Twins*

_____ copy/copies of *Affair of the Heart*

_____ copy/copies of *Swede*

Other:

_____ copy/copies of *Slickfester Dude Tells Bedtime Stories*

> For more information or to be added to our mailing list, call or fax us on our toll-free number
> **1-888-551-0973**

> **SPECIAL OFFER:** Order 3 or more items, we'll pay the shipping.

Name _____

Address _____

City _____ State _____

Zip _____ Phone # _____

_____ Book(s) at $9.95 = Total $ _____

Add $3 postage/handling if only one item
Add $5 postage/handling if two items _____

**WE PAY SHIPPING/HANDLING IF
ordering three or more items!**

Total enclosed $ _____

Make checks payable to WillowSpring Downs and mail, along with this order form, to the following address:

**WillowSpring Downs
1582 Falcon
Hillsboro, KS 67063-9600**